forever FOUR

· staying in tune ·

GROSSET & DUNLAP
Published by the Penguin Group
Penguin Group (USA) Inc., 375 Hudson Street,
New York, New York 10014, USA
Penguin Group (Canada), 90 Eglinton Avenue East, Suite 700, Toronto,
Ontario M4P 2Y3, Canada (a division of Pearson Penguin Canada Inc.)
Penguin Books Ltd, 80 Strand, London WC2R 0RL, England
Penguin Ireland, 25 St Stephen's Green, Dublin 2, Ireland
(a division of Penguin Books Ltd)
Penguin Group (Australia), 707 Collins Street, Melbourne, Victoria 3008,
Australia (a division of Pearson Australia Group Pty Ltd)
Penguin Books India Pvt Ltd, 11 Community Centre,
Panchsheel Park, New Delhi—110 017, India
Penguin Group (NZ), 67 Apollo Drive, Rosedale,
Auckland 0632, New Zealand (a division of Pearson New Zealand Ltd)
Penguin Books, Rosebank Office Park, 181 Jan Smuts Avenue,
Parktown North 2193, South Africa
Penguin China, B7 Jaiming Center, 27 East Third Ring Road North,
Chaoyang District, Beijing 100020, China

Penguin Books Ltd, Registered Offices:
80 Strand, London WC2R 0RL, England

Text copyright © 2013 by Elizabeth Cody Kimmel. Illustrations
copyright © 2013 by Penguin Group (USA) Inc. All rights reserved. Published
by Grosset & Dunlap, a division of Penguin Young Readers Group,
345 Hudson Street, New York, New York 10014. GROSSET & DUNLAP
is a trademark of Penguin Group (USA) Inc. Printed in the U.S.A.

Library of Congress Control Number: 2012024486

ISBN 978-0-448-45551-8 (pbk)   10 9 8 7 6 5 4 3 2 1
ISBN 978-0-448-46329-2 (hc)   10 9 8 7 6 5 4 3 2 1

ALWAYS LEARNING   **PEARSON**

forever FOUR

· staying in tune ·

by Elizabeth Cody Kimmel
Grosset & Dunlap
An Imprint of Penguin Group (USA) Inc.

For Nigel and Sibyl—ECK

· chapter ·
1

I felt a ripple of excitement as the auditorium lights dimmed and Miko Suzuki walked confidently onto the stage, her violin in one hand. In the seat next to me, Tally Janeway was nervously wiggling her foot. At the sight of our friend raising the violin to her chin, Tally's foot wiggling doubled in speed and intensity. On my other side, my best friend, Ivy Scanlon, was watching Miko intently, her pale-blue eyes shining with anticipation. I took a deep breath as a white-haired woman followed Miko onstage and sat at the keyboard of a grand piano. The audience fell completely silent.

I felt as excited as Ivy looked and as nervous as Tally's jiggling foot indicated she was. The four of us had been spending a lot of time with each other since coming together to create *4 Girls* magazine back in September. Though I'd always known Miko was superserious about playing the violin, I'd never actually heard her play. That was all about to change.

Miko looked gorgeous in a red velvet dress with a black flower sewn on the right shoulder. Her glossy black hair was pulled back from her face with shiny silver clips. Miko always looked great, but tonight there was something different. Something WONDERFUL. She seemed to fill the entire stage with her presence. *Maybe that's what confidence looks like*, I thought.

Tucking her violin under her chin, Miko raised the bow over the strings, her eyes trained on the pianist. The woman at the piano gave a small nod, played a few notes on the keys, and then it was all Miko.

My mouth dropped open slightly as Miko pulled the bow across the strings and the most AMAZING sound filled the auditorium. One part tuneful whine, one part soul, and a whole lot of emotion came through in just a few notes. I'd never sat down and really listened to a violin solo before, but now I would try to pick that heartfelt sound out of every orchestral ensemble I heard for the rest of my life. Next to me, I heard Tally give a quiet sigh. The song was sweet and nostalgic. I'd listened to the short tune, called *Salut d'Amour*, on my iPod a few times after Miko had told me it was one of the pieces she would be playing. But as I watched my friend play the familiar notes with her own hands, I felt my breath catch in my throat. There was a brief silence as Miko finished the song and lowered her violin.

Then the auditorium filled with the sound of applause.

"I knew she was good, but I had no idea she was *that* good," Ivy exclaimed.

"Right?" I said, clapping hard, balancing the bouquet of roses I'd brought on my lap. "She played it perfectly. Now she plays the second piece—the one by Bach."

Miko stood still, acknowledging the audience with a small smile. I stopped clapping and held my hands clasped tightly in my lap. I had asked Miko incessantly about proper behavior at a classical music concert. I'd heard that there were certain times when you were supposed to clap politely and other times you were supposed to wait. Miko had explained that if you were listening to a long piece like a sonata or a symphony, you shouldn't applaud during the brief pauses between movements, but it was okay to clap for a few moments when one piece ended and before a new one began.

When Miko raised the violin to her chin again, everyone fell silent. I knew this piece, too. It was called *Ave Maria*. I hummed along silently inside my head as Miko played the familiar tune. Her eyes were closed slightly, and her brow furrowed in concentration. Miko's right hand, carefully holding her bow over the strings, looked both strong and graceful. The song ended with a long, low note.

Miko opened her eyes, lowered her violin again, and took a bow. I began to clap wildly.

"Bravo!" Tally was calling. "Encore!"

"Yes, encore!" I cried, echoing Tally, but the applause was so loud I'm sure Miko couldn't hear us all the way up on the stage.

Miko gave another bow, then gestured toward the pianist, who stood and took a bow, too. Then Miko walked offstage, taking graceful steps in heels so high I probably could not have even stood still in them without tottering.

There were two other performers in the program. One was a boy around Miko's age, and one was a girl several years older. They both played pieces by Mozart. If I had only come to hear the two of them, I would have been impressed by the fact that they could play at all. But following Miko's performance, I could hear some subtle and some not-so-subtle mistakes in each of their songs, and places where they weren't quite in tune. *Miko has really got something special*, I thought as the lights came up in the auditorium. I followed Ivy and Tally to the lobby, superexcited to see our friend and applaud her performance in person.

"Can you guys believe how good she was?" I exclaimed, the roses tucked under my arm. "I'm a little nervous to see her right now."

"Ivy, text her again!" Tally said impatiently. "What if she goes out the stage door and we don't see her?"

Ivy laughed. "Tal, this isn't Carnegie Hall," she said. "She'll come out the same door as everyone else. Besides, her parents are standing right over there. You think she's going to leave without them?"

I looked around, wondering if anyone else from school had come. Since Miko was one of the most popular girls in our grade, I wouldn't be surprised to see a few familiar faces. I hoped we weren't going to run into Shelby Simpson, though. Since she was Miko's best friend, she was most likely around somewhere. Then I caught sight of the violinist herself.

"Oh, guys, I see her!" I said.

Miko had come into the lobby and headed straight for her parents. Her mother gave her a big hug and her father began talking and waving his hands around while Miko nodded.

"The transitions have to be more crisp in Bach, Miko," he was saying. "There's a difference between holding back and just sounding like you don't know the piece you are playing."

Whoa. I wondered what performance Miko's dad

had seen because I was pretty sure it wasn't the same one *I'd* seen. Miko had sounded spectacular to me.

"And you have to make that legato smoother while still leaving a break between the two notes," he continued. "We've talked about this before."

Miko was looking at the floor, chewing her lower lip and nodding.

"But your bowing was perfect, and you played with such sensitivity, Miko," her mother said. "I love it when you play like that—so sophisticated, and I can hear the emotion in the piece. Smoothing out those transitions will be easy for you to fix."

"Thanks, Mom," Miko said.

"Yes, that aspect was excellent. But back to the issue of contrasts, Miko," her father continued. Then he leaned in closer, and I couldn't hear what he was saying any longer.

Miko caught my eye for a fraction of a second, still nodding as she listened to her father. When he paused to take a breath, Miko pointed our way. Her mother turned, and when she spotted us across the room, she waved and gave Miko a little nudge. Miko rushed over to where we were waiting.

"You guys are so great to come to my recital," Miko said.

I laughed. "Of course we would come," I told her.

"You've been working toward this for so long. You blew us away up there!"

"That music was *sooo* romantic," Tally declared. "Especially the first song. What was it again?"

"Elgar's *Salut d'Amour*," Miko said.

"It is actually a love song," I said. "Elgar wrote it as an engagement present for his fiancée."

"Wow, Paulie, you've really done your homework," Miko said, looking impressed.

Tally drew in a deep breath and clasped her hands together in front of her heart. "Oh, wouldn't you just die if someone wrote a song like that for you? I would cry every time I heard it for the rest of my life, no matter how old I got to be. And if I couldn't hear the song, I would just say the name over and over again. *Salut d'Amour. Salut d'Amour. Salut d'Amour.*"

"Oh, I almost forgot! These are for you—from all three of us," I said, handing Miko the bouquet of bright-red roses.

"They're beautiful," Miko said warmly. "Thank you so much!" She smiled at us, then glanced around the room for a moment, like she was looking for someone else.

"You deserve them, Miko, really. You sounded like a pro," Ivy said.

Miko looked embarrassed. "Oh, guys, come

on. It's not *that* hard of a piece. I did get through with no mistakes, but my dad's right, it was still far from perfect."

"It sounded perfect to *me*," I said. "Both pieces did. And you played them without reading the music! It must have taken you forever to learn them by heart."

Miko laughed. "Oh, you'd be amazed," she said. "Forever is more like three weeks. A pro could learn those songs in a day or two, though. Seriously, guys, I'm a long way from the big leagues, according to my dad."

"Don't be so humble," I said, giving Miko a nudge. "We've personally witnessed you wowing the big leagues, remember?"

Ivy's mother had arranged for us to go to New York City over Thanksgiving break to do a special web edition of *4 Girls* from inside one of the most famous magazines there was: *City Nation*. Miko had impressed the managing editor and the entire design department with her keen eye for style. The managing editor, Garamond, had encouraged her to apply for one of the coveted summer internships and even offered to coach her on getting her application just right.

"Speaking of which, any news on the internship?" Ivy asked. "Have you talked to Garamond again?"

"It's looking pretty impossible at this point," Miko

said. "My dad saw the application Garamond sent, and he kind of went ballistic. He said the city is too far away to commute every day, and if I was staying there, one of my parents would have to stay, too. I mean, I'd love to do it—it would be like a dream come true. But Dad is really pushing for the Music Conservatory program this summer, which would be a different kind of amazing. I wish I could do them both. But since the Music Conservatory is closer to home, I think I'm going to have to tell Garamond that I just can't apply for the *City Nation* internship. It's fine."

I looked at Miko carefully. Something in her tone didn't sound *fine*. Miko never backed down from a challenge. At least, not before she had all the information in front of her. If she didn't *get* the *City Nation* internship, then she could still focus on the Music Conservatory. But to not even try? I was starting to wonder just how much Miko's father was influencing her choices.

"Did you get accepted by the conservatory already?" Tally asked.

"Not yet," Miko said. "I submitted the application. The musical audition and music-theory exam are in just over two weeks. I'm going to have to practice every spare minute I have from now until then, and my dad got me an audition coach to prepare for the music-theory exam. I was hoping to create another original cover for the next *4 Girls* issue, but I'm not going to have time. I'm going to have to be on extralight duty this time. Again! I'm so sorry."

"You have nothing to be sorry about," I assured her. "We'll just do what we did before, on issue number two. You help us out when you can and let us know when you can't. We'll get it all done. We don't even need the next issue completed for another two and a half weeks. That's the great thing about making it a winter issue instead of a December issue—we ended up with some extra time!"

"And with all the requests we've had on the blog for people to be able to contribute their own work, we're thinking the whole theme is going to be kind of like a collaboration between *4 Girls* and our readers. That's what we were going to call it—Collaboration Concepts. All the contributions will mean there is less work for us all to do this time around," Ivy chimed in. "We have plenty of time."

"Okay, good," Miko said, looking relieved. "I'm totally on board for the helping out and going to meetings when I can. I told my parents that *4 Girls* is as much a priority for me as this conservatory audition is for them."

"Speaking of your parents, here comes your mom," Ivy said.

Miko's mother was a petite, elegant-looking woman in a deep-blue pantsuit, her graying hair pulled up in a bun.

"Hi, Mrs. Suzuki," I said.

"Hi, girls," Mrs. Suzuki said. "Tally, Ivy, Paulina, it's so nice to see you here supporting Miko. Thank you for coming. Have you girls seen Shelby?"

"I haven't seen her," I said, looking around. "Maybe she's looking for Miko back in the auditorium? Anyway, we wouldn't have missed this for the world! We haven't seen enough of Miko lately. She's been so busy. But guess what, Meek—my mom says I can have some friends over for New Year's. Can you come?"

Miko looked quickly at her mother, but Mrs. Suzuki was already shaking her head.

"That's very nice of you," Mrs. Suzuki said. "But Miko's father has a friend visiting us that night who is a very successful pianist. He thinks it would be helpful for Miko to talk to him."

"On New Year's Eve?" Miko said. "Was Dad even going to ask me about this, or is it all decided?"

"I thought he had," Mrs. Suzuki said. "He thought you'd be excited about it."

Miko said nothing, but turned her face slightly away from her mother and rolled her eyes a little.

"Sorry, Paulie," Miko told me. "I would have loved

to have gone to your house. I guess the three of you will have to ring in the new year without me."

"Oh, I can't go, either," Tally said. "The whole Drama Club is going to Buster's cousin's house. His parents are pastry chefs! We're going to eat like kings and queens! Tea cakes and petit fours and meringues and raspberry cheesecake tarts!"

"Are you serious?" Miko asked. "That's so cool. My favorite dessert in the world is strawberry creamed—"

"Sweetheart, your father is waiting," Mrs. Suzuki interrupted. "We're supposed to go out for coffee with your teacher to talk about your performance, remember?"

I could see Miko's father looking impatient. He kept glancing at his watch. *Poor Miko*, I thought. *Why couldn't he let her enjoy being with her friends for just five minutes?*

Miko sighed softly. "I'd better go. You guys, seriously, thanks so much for coming. It means . . . a lot."

"An alien invasion could not have kept me away," Tally declared. "Actually, I wouldn't be surprised if we ran into an alien invasion on the way home. I saw this TV show about this race of space people that are hypnotized by the sound of string instruments. It's like some kind of communication or something for them because they used to be whales, and they're used to talking to the whales in our ocean, which sounds like violin music, and if they happen to be passing close enough to a concert, they steer the spaceship straight for—"

"Tal, she's gotta go," I said gently. Tally's stories could go on all night, and Miko was out of time.

Miko's mother walked toward Mr. Suzuki, making a little "hurry up" gesture to Miko. She quickly scanned the room like she was hoping to see somebody else—probably Shelby—in the crowd. Her shoulders slumped a little when she didn't find her.

"Thanks again for coming, you guys," Miko said. She gave us each a quick hug. "And if I don't talk to you before, have a great New Year's! Can you believe we only have less than a week until school starts again?"

"I can't believe it," I said. "It seems like we just went on break. See you later, Miko. And great job, again."

As Miko rejoined her parents, my phone beeped, and I checked the screen.

I'm outside. Are you ready to go?

"Hey, guys, my mom's waiting for us," I said.

Tally zipped up her coat—a massive, ankle-length down jacket that she completely disappeared into. I

13

had learned many things about Tally Janeway, future famous actress, and one of them was that she simply could not stand to be cold.

"I'm ready," Ivy said. She had on a simple navy wool coat and a blue-and-white-striped scarf. If Tally was the picture of extravagance, Ivy was the exact opposite. Simplicity was her style, vintage simplicity whenever possible.

"One second," Tally said, fumbling in her enormous purse and pulling out two fat mittens, a scarf, and a purple-and-green wool hat with two long, hanging strings that looked like hat pigtails.

Ivy tried to hide the small smile pulling at her lips as Tally pulled the hat over her mass of wild blond curls and yanked it down as far as it would go without covering her eyes. Then she rummaged through her purse and pulled out something that looked like an electric hand warmer.

"My mom is right outside," I told Tally. "We don't have far to walk. And the car will be heated."

Tally looked like she suspected some reality show producer was going to drop her in the wilderness and film her making her way back to civilization through the snowdrifts with only the clothes on her back and the supplies in her purse. *Though if it was going to happen to one person in the world*, I thought, *that person would be Tally Janeway.*

"*Your* version of heat is different than *my* version of heat," Tally insisted. "The weather report this morning said it was going to be thirty below zero today!"

"Um, I believe the actual report said thirty degrees," Ivy corrected her. "When they don't specify, they mean above zero."

"It's like the South Pole out there," Tally said. "It sure feels like thirty below."

She sighed and looked ruefully toward the exit, like a polar explorer about to leave her hut. "Okay, I'm ready," Tally said, her voice slightly muffled since her chin and lips were covered by the collar of her coat.

"Are you absolutely sure?" Ivy asked playfully. "I can still see your nose."

Tally wrapped her scarf around her head so that only her eyes were visible above it. Then she nodded.

As we headed out the door, I caught my breath as a blast of wind hit me. It *was* pretty cold out! The wind made the skin on my face tingle. But as promised, my mother was waiting in a warm car right outside the concert hall with my little brother, Kevin, in the front seat.

As Tally, Ivy, and I squished into the backseat, it hit me how sad I was that Miko wasn't with us. I was superexcited for her that the concert went so well and that she had an audition at the conservatory, but at the same time I felt bad. I'd always known Miko's dad could really put the pressure on her to be perfect. But with this audition coming up, I had a feeling Miko was going to be even more stressed out at home than usual. Her parents weren't going to let her spend much time on anything besides her music. Including us.

· chapter · 2

"Have you heard from Miko, Paulie? I haven't since the concert, and that was three days ago," Ivy said, reclining on my couch. She wore a comfy-looking sweater jacket decorated with a vintage pin that said HAPPY NEW YEAR!

"I called her yesterday," I said, "but we only talked for a few minutes. Her dad kept interrupting to ask her when she was going to practice, and finally we just gave up. I asked again if she could get over here tonight at some point just for a little while, but she can't get out of dinner with her parents' friend. I was really hoping the four of us could spend New Year's together."

"Well, Tally's got her theater party, anyway," Ivy said. "But it's a bummer that Miko's stuck with her parents and some pianist. Any idea what Benny's up to tonight?"

I sighed, shaking my head. "I have no idea," I said. "Honestly, Ivy, I'm not really sure what's going on. I'm getting really freaked out now. I told you he texted me right before Christmas that he was really sick, but when he was better he had a present he wanted to give to me, right?"

"Yeah. Wait, though. That's not the last time you heard from him, is it?" Ivy asked.

I nodded. "It is. Christmas was a week ago! You figure with a bad case of strep, you're out of it for maybe four or five days, right? But it's been seven!"

"So why not just call him?" Ivy asked. It was not the first time she had suggested this. But it also wouldn't be the last time I didn't follow her advice. Even though we'd been "dating" since the end of September, there were still times when I experienced a spectacular lack of confidence where Benny Novak was concerned. I turned into what Ivy called the Anxiety Blob. I'd get worried that he'd met another girl he liked better or that I'd accidentally done something incredibly horrible and made him mad. Or my worst-case, try-not-to-think-about-it scenario. After dating me for a while, he'd just realized he didn't like me all that much.

"I'd feel stupid calling him," I said. "He specifically said he would call ME about bringing the present by when he was better. And he never called. I can't just dial his number and be like, 'So, hey, where's this present?' There's no way for me to know if something's going on or if he got even sicker or if he's just lost interest for some reason."

"Paulina. Benny Novak has *not* lost interest in you," Ivy said firmly.

"Well, then what happened to him?" I asked.

Ivy shook her head. "I don't know. But like I keep telling you, I don't think it's weird for you to just shoot him a text message and *ask*. You know, something like—'So did you survive the dreaded strep throat, or should I be shopping for a black dress for your funeral?'"

"I know." I sighed. "I'm just being a wimp about it. I feel like he said he would be in touch when he was feeling better, and it would be clingy or whatever to nag. I know, I know—if I'm not going to take your advice, I should just stop complaining."

"Complain all you want," Ivy said, nudging me with her socked foot. "It's just you and me tonight. And that's what best friends are for."

"Don't forget me!" my little brother said as he walked into the room with a glass of eggnog in his hand. "And I don't want to hear about Beennnnnnny Nooooooovak lovey-dovey stuff. Blech. Look what Mom gave me."

"Eggnog," Ivy said. "Yum."

"Is there really nog in it?" Kevin asked, peering into the glass of creamy liquid.

"It's just called eggnog," I told Kevin. "It's a traditional holiday drink. I don't think *nog* is really a word."

"Yes, it is!" exclaimed Kevin. "Nog is a Ferengi! He's Quark's nephew. He was the first Ferengi to go to Starfleet Academy. That's the only reason I wanted to try this stuff in the first place."

"*Star Trek*," Ivy explained, noticing the mystified look on my face.

"Okay," I replied, nodding.

"You know, you could be onto something," Ivy told Kevin. "Eggnog might have originated as a delicacy among the Ferengi. Maybe Nog discovered it, and they named it after him."

"Also, it's packed with sugar," I said.

Kevin looked from Ivy to me. Then he took a small, cautious sip. "Wow," he said, his eyes large and his upper lip coated in white. "It is sweet."

"You'll be bouncing around the room soon," Ivy said, winking at me. "They could use you to power the warp engines of the Starship *Enterprise*."

"Make that glass last," my mother said, coming into the living room with a plate of cookies. "That's the only one you're going to get."

"Luke Zimmerman says there's rum in eggnog and

that's what pirates drink," Kevin stated.

"There's no rum in *that* eggnog," my mother said. "But I'm not expecting any pirates this evening, so I think it's okay." She gave me and Ivy a wink.

"I've got a few things to finish up in the kitchen, then I'll be back in," my mom said. "Give a shout if you guys need anything, okay?"

"Thanks, Mrs. Barbosa," Ivy said.

When my mother was out of the room, Ivy nudged me. "I'm kind of amazed," she said. "Your mom is sort of world famous for her superhealthy snacks. What happened to the tofu cubes she put out the first time we had a *4 Girls* meeting here?"

I laughed. "Oh, she's gotten a teeny bit better, but basically she hasn't changed when it comes to snacks. She just makes an exception for the holidays. She likes to go all out now that it's just the three of us. Once school starts again, the tofu snacks will be back!"

"So can we watch the New Year's Eve *Star Trek* marathon?" Kevin asked, giving me a pleading look. "Ivy wants to, right, Ivy?"

"You know I love *Star Trek*," Ivy said truthfully. "It's up to Paulina, though. It is a great show, Paulie."

"*Pleeeeeease?*" Kevin begged.

"It's fine with me," I said. I'd already been planning to do more talking to Ivy and checking Facebook to see if Benny had posted any status updates than actual TV watching, anyway.

"Yay!" Kevin yelled, grabbing the remote. "Death to the Klingons! Hail, Captain Kirk! Spock rocks!"

"I wonder if Tally is at her party yet," I said.

"She is probably at *a* party," Ivy said. "But is she at the right party? Can you totally imagine her going to the wrong house and not even noticing for, like, an hour? I swear, the cold weather is making her even more scatterbrained than usual, if such a thing is possible."

"I know, right? Like last week when she spent twenty minutes sitting in the Mexican restaurant in the mall when we were downstairs waiting for her in the Chinese place?"

"And it was *her* idea to meet for tea and eggrolls," Ivy added. "How many Mexican restaurants do you know that serve those?"

Ivy and I had set our phones together on the table in front of us. In perfect unison, both phones pinged, and we reached for them at the same time.

"Miko," Ivy said.

"Mine too."

> Hey, guys—have a blast tonight. Sorry I can't be there with you. My dad's pianist friend is actually kind of interesting, and we're all heading out to dinner at La Piccolina. Yum!

"I hope she means it," Ivy said. "I can't believe her parents are making her hang with their friend tonight."

"I have a feeling we're not going to see that much of Miko until after her audition," I said as I typed a quick text back.

We miss you! Hope ur having fun!

"Well, we'll see her at school, anyway," Ivy said. "It's not like she'll be missing *that* to practice."

"You never know," I said. "Her dad was pretty intense at the concert. I almost feel bad that she'll be helping us with *4 Girls* at all in her free time. Maybe we should just tell her to take the entire issue off."

"Don't feel bad," Ivy told me. "Miko is amazing at designing the magazine, and we both know she loves doing it. She said she wants to help. And you know Miko—if she can't do something, she'll come right out and say it."

"That's true," I said. "At some point, though, we are going to have to figure out what to do about a cover."

Ivy snapped her fingers.

"Oh, that reminds me," she said. "I had an idea about that. What if we held a competition of our own for a piece of artwork to put on the cover. It makes perfect sense, since the whole theme of the issue is Collaboration Concepts—readers working with us, instead of just reading the finished product. We could put the word out on the blog asking people to submit something they've created—original art, a photograph, a digital design, anything really. We'll pick the winner, and that'll be our cover."

"That's a great idea," I agreed. "Maybe Miko would be able to help us judge the entries, too. All four of us could do it, but Miko could be the head judge since she's our designer. That would probably only take one meeting to do. If she knows far enough in advance, it shouldn't cut into her music time too much."

"Definitely," Ivy said. "And we can tell people they have to submit anonymously. That way it doesn't get personal."

"I agree," I said. "And it's great because it gives our readers a way to have more input in the actual magazine instead of just the blog."

"You guys, come on. Stop talking. The show's about to start!" Kevin said, pointing at the television. He took a sip of his eggnog, jumped up, zoomed out of the room shouting, "Mom, do you want to watch *Star Trek*?" then shot back in a second later.

"She has to finish rolling out the pie crust," he said, huffing and puffing a little. "Then she's going to come in."

"I'm definitely ready for some *Star Trek*," Ivy said.

"Ivy, who's your favorite character?" Kevin asked as he grabbed a pillow from the couch and plopped it on the floor right in front of the TV.

"Dr. McCoy," Ivy said.

"Mine's Spock," Kevin said. "But you're a girl, so you should have a girl favorite character. It should be Lieutenant Uhura or Nurse Chapel."

"Girls don't have to just have girl favorite characters," Ivy pointed out.

"Yes, they do," Kevin shot back.

"But *I'm* a girl, and *my* favorite character is a *boy*," Ivy said. "How do you, explain that?"

"That doesn't count 'cause McCoy is the doctor," Kevin said, flopping down on his stomach and propping himself up on the pillow.

"Uh-huh," Ivy said, smiling at me. "Doctors don't count as boys. When you explain it like that, of course it makes perfect sense."

I smiled back, getting more comfortable on the couch and taking a sip of my eggnog. My New Year's Eve plan wasn't glamorous or adventuresome, but I wasn't much for parties or loud celebrations. Staying curled up on the couch with my best friend and permission to stay up past midnight was the best New Year's Eve for me. It would have been perfect if Miko and Tally had come, too. *Maybe next year*, I thought with a sigh. Would Benny Novak be speaking to me by then? Would he have a new girlfriend? Would we still be publishing *4 Girls* a year from now? I couldn't imagine life without it, or without the four of us together. And the thought of Benny going out with a different girl made me feel nauseous. I chased the thought from my mind.

"It's nine o'clock," Ivy observed. "We're really getting down to the wire. In three hours, it will be next year!"

"It happens so fast," I said. "It always makes me feel weird when it gets close to the final countdown, like it's my last chance to do something THIS year, you know?"

"Like text Benny Novak?" Ivy joked.

"Stop," I said. "I'm not going to do it, not tonight."

"Okay, it's starting. Nobody make any noise!" Kevin yelled.

Ivy reached for the plate of cookies and took two, handing one to me.

"Happy New Year, bestie," she said.

"Happy New Year!" I replied.

"Shhh!" Kevin looked like he was about to explode.

I took a big bite of cookie. I planned on talking to Ivy all night about everything—*4 Girls*, Miko's concert, our big Thanksgiving trip to Manhattan, whether Benny Novak was now my ex-boyfriend after only a couple months of going out. That was the great thing about having a best friend—you could talk about the same thing over and over again, and they stuck right in there with you. I wanted to see if Ivy thought there was another girl Benny might like—if she'd noticed anything at all before Christmas break.

But for now, I settled for a mouthful of cookie and the opening theme to Kevin's favorite show.

It was going to be a happy new year, indeed. It had to be. And I was sure everything else would work itself out eventually.

· chapter ·

3

I sat in the waiting room with my toes pointed together while a tiny blond girl dressed head to toe in a pink rayon leopard-print sweat suit slammed two toys together. I rummaged in my purse for my iPod and sighed with irritation when I realized I had forgotten it. It had been so nice to have Christmas break away from school. If it hadn't been for Benny Novak disappearing off the radar, it would have been a perfect vacation. Ten whole school-free days! What a bummer to have to spend the very last day of it in an orthodontist's office!

My January 2 appointment had been looming like a zombie in a closet forever. Now it was here. The zombie almost had the door off the hinges and soon the nightmare would be upon me. I tried not to think about the fact that in an hour or so I would have braces. Was I going to look like a complete loser? If

Benny by some remote chance reappeared, would he take one look at me and run away screaming?

I put those thoughts out of my mind for the twentieth time that day, relieved my mother had agreed to let me wait by myself, so I wouldn't have to talk to anyone. *Think about* 4 Girls, I told myself, *and get a little work done.* I turned on my phone and read over an e-mail from Ivy.

▼ **To:** Paulina M. Barbosa, Fashion Maven, StarQuality

▼ **From:** IvyNYC

▼ **Subject:** (none)

Ok, guys, this is my first official act as submissions coordinator. We've received two poems, a really gossipy essay I don't see how we can possibly use, and a review of the cafeteria menu that is actually pretty hilarious. Paulina, here's a question—are we going to just accept or reject stuff, or are we going to do any editing work on them? Also, good luck today!

I reread Ivy's e-mail several times, weighing the pros and cons of attempting to edit my fellow students' work, but I just couldn't concentrate. The little girl in pink was now running in circles around the waiting room, making a noise like a helicopter. *Where were her parents?* I scowled at her, and she giggled maniacally.

To make matters worse, a television mounted on the wall was tuned in to the Food Network, and a perky woman with helmet hair and a kitchen-inappropriate shiny gold tunic shirt was loudly discussing the secret to a foolproof low-fat chocolate mousse. I gave the e-mail one last try, but it was like the Food Network lady and the little girl were conspiring to stop me from focusing. I decided to open a text from Tally.

hppf ;ivl ypfsu hryyomh yjr ntsvrd!!!

Tally frequently had difficulty managing the little keyboard on her phone. I tried to decipher her message, but could make neither head nor tail of even the first word.

"Oh, forget it," I muttered, tossing my phone back into my purse.

"Forget it!" the little girl screamed, her blond, pink-ribboned pigtails quivering as she imitated me. I was seriously considering sticking my tongue out at her, when the door leading to the various exam rooms opened. I looked up expectantly, then did a double take.

"Shelby!" I said in surprise.

Shelby Simpson, unrivaled leader of the girls I secretly called Prom-Queens-in-Training, also happened to be Miko's oldest and closest friend. Though we weren't exactly enemies, it was no secret that Shelby and I really didn't like each other very much. But it would be rude to pretend like I hadn't seen her when I obviously had, since I'd just said her name out loud. So I got up and walked over to her.

"Oh, hey, Shelby. So you're getting braces, too, huh? Are you as totally excited as I am?" I asked with a laugh.

As usual, Shelby looked totally together, not a blond hair out of place, wearing skinny jeans and a long turquoise cashmere sweater jacket with tiny dangling earrings that matched the color precisely. She was so perfect looking, it was hard to imagine her with train tracks on her teeth. I have to say, I felt a tiny sense of relief that I wasn't the only one just starting with braces. Several girls in my grade had had theirs for a year already. Shelby looked surprised for a moment, like my question made absolutely no sense. Her surprise was all just an act, I knew, her way of showing that she was more important than me—at least to herself. We were in an orthodontist's office, after all; obviously braces were involved.

"Oh, you're getting those metal brackets on your

teeth," she said suddenly, with a tone of sympathy that I was sure was fake.

"Well, yeah, that's kind of what braces are, right?" I asked.

"Not for everybody," Shelby said. "They gave me these clear plastic things that fit right over your teeth. They're totally invisible. Lots more expensive, of course. But so worth it, I mean, who wants to walk around with clunky hardware in their mouth, right? It's like you wouldn't be able to eat in public or go out on a date or anything. Do people even still get the old-fashioned kind?"

Ugh. I wanted to wipe the satisfied smile right off her face. Instead, I gave her my most cheerful smile.

"Yep, that's me, old-fashioned all the way. What can I say—I go for the classic look. Miko is starting to rub off on me that way."

"Hmmm," Shelby said, looking over my shoulder as if there might be someone more interesting in the waiting room to talk to.

"Speaking of Miko and classic, she just blew everyone's socks off at that recital, don't you think?"

Shelby's face darkened slightly. "Yeah, well, I had family in town that day. It's not like I could just blow them off. I didn't have a ride."

Ah. So Shelby really hadn't been at the recital. I thought maybe I'd just missed seeing her, but then I remembered Miko searching the crowds for someone she couldn't find.

"Oh no, yeah, I mean, I'm sure Miko understood. You guys are best friends, after all. I'm sure she was fine with it."

Shelby's face reddened suddenly, and she scowled and looked away. She pulled out her phone and stared at it, like she was expecting it to ring. Then she pressed a speed-dial button.

"Hey, Meeky, it's Shel," she said, leveling a cool gaze at me, then looking away again. "Did you see Daphne's Facebook status? You totally predicted she would do that, remember? I'm . . . sorry, what's starting right now?"

Miko had an extra violin lesson on Tuesday afternoons. They'd been scheduled for the last six weeks. How could Shelby not know that?

"No, that's cool. Just check it out when you get home, then call me. Later!"

Shelby tossed the phone into her purse. She took a step toward the door, then stopped and looked at me. "So Miko and I were talking the other day about that cover competition you're having," she said.

"Yep," I said.

"Well, I'm going to be entering," Shelby said, lifting her eyebrows like she was daring me to have a problem with that.

"Oh," I said. Shelby usually acted like she and her PQuit friends were way too cool for our lame little magazine. And as far as I knew, she didn't have an artistic bone in her body. But if she wanted to enter, there was nothing anyone could do to stop her.

"I already know what I'm going to do," Shelby told me.

"That's good, but don't tell me," I said. "We're actually going to ask people to submit anonymously so we have no idea what submission came from who."

"Well, you'll know which one is mine as soon as you see it," Shelby said. "At least, Miko will."

Her phone chirped, and she glanced at the screen.

"My ride's here," she said, turning on her heel and heading for the door.

"Bye," I called after her.

"Byyyyyyyyyyye," said the little girl in pigtails, who was standing behind me looking sticky.

"Paulina Barbosa?" called an official-sounding voice.

The moment of truth had arrived.

"Right here," I said.

A woman in blue scrubs stood by the door to the exam room, beaming.

"Come on in," she said cheerfully.

I would have preferred it if she had NOT sounded quite so happy.

"Okay," I said, pushing a button on my phone to bring up my mother's contact.

> **Mom, I'm going in now. They said it would take around an hour, so see you then. Thanks for letting me go solo. When you see me, pretend I don't look different!**

I turned the phone off and followed the world's happiest orthodontist into the exam room. As I walked, I wondered for the fiftieth time that day how I would look with braces, how I would eat with braces, how I would sleep with braces, and perhaps most important, whether Benny Novak would ever ask me out again once I had them.

· chapter ·

4

The first day back at school after Christmas break was always hard for me. It was the longest vacation we got during the school year, but it always seemed like such a letdown to go back to the daily grind after all the parties and holiday feasts. It was also kind of confusing to start back at school on a Wednesday, in the middle of the week. The only good part about it was the shift in schedules—no more second-period health. Now I had art, which sounded a whole lot better. Plus, Miko, Tally, and Ivy had art, too—the first time all four of us had a class together.

"We didn't have an art class at my school in New York City," Ivy told me as we walked down the hall together. "It got totally cut from the budget. What do we do, finger-paint? Glue glitter on stuff?"

I laughed. "I think we're a little past that," I told

her. "But the art teacher is new. I haven't heard anything about her. So I have no idea what to expect."

"So it could be finger painting, then," Ivy said.

"If you want to finger-paint, Ivy, I'm sure that can be worked out," I assured her with a grin as we walked into the brightly lit art room.

We were early, which meant we had our pick of seats. I headed for a round table near the big window in the back of the room. Outside, we could see the wind blowing swirls of snow into the air and the trees heavy with icicles.

"Oh, perfect," Ivy said. "That sun feels so good. I can't believe how cold it is outside. Hey, did you read the competition announcement I put on the blog? I printed it, too."

Blogpost: Calling All Artists!
Posted by: 4Girls

Hey, *4 Girls* readers—we've gotten so many great submissions for this month's issue, we've decided to take it one step further. We want one of YOU to create the cover of the next *4 Girls*! Here's how it will work: If you have or want to create a painting, photograph, drawing, collage, digital design, or anything you think would make an awesome *4 Girls* cover, submit it to us at this special e-mail

"This looks great," I said. "Thanks for doing it. I
meant to go online and look last night, but my mouth
hurt so much there was nothing to do but go to bed
two hours early."

"Seriously, the braces look fine, Paulie," Ivy said.
"And I love that you can pick colors for the bands.
Purple suits you."

"Ugh," I said, putting my hand over my mouth. "I
feel like a fool. My lips look different now—they sort
of pooch out a little. And I'm definitely not talking
right. I think I have a little lisp."

"Honestly, you don't sound any different," Ivy
said. "I'm sure it feels really strange to talk right
now, but you'll get used to it."

"Easy for you to say," I told my friend. Like Miko,

Ivy had a perfect smile and would not need to go through the agony of braces.

"Oh my gosh, will you please look at Tally?" Ivy said, nodding her head toward the door.

Tally was strolling into the art room wearing a sweater so huge she looked like a walking marshmallow. She had a pair of fat boots covered in white fake fur that looked like they had come from some prehistoric snow creature, and the outfit was topped off by a purple wool scarf wrapped three times around her neck.

"Tal, come sit here," I called to her, laughing. "We have a nice, sunny table."

"Oh, y'all," she said, hurrying over and throwing an overstuffed book bag onto the floor next to a chair. "I thought I was going to die waiting for the bus this morning. My lips were so numb I couldn't talk for half of first period."

"I'd have to see that to believe it," Ivy said. "I didn't think there was any force in the known universe that could slow you down when you had something to say."

"No, it's true!" Tally insisted. "Audriana asked me if I'd just come from the dentist. She thought I'd had a shot of novocaine. One time I went to the dentist and he gave me too much novocaine, and on the way home my mother picked up some fried chicken, and my mouth kept watering, but my lips couldn't hold it in, so I was drooling everywhere, but I couldn't feel it because my face was numb, and—"

"Ew!" Ivy said, laughing and shaking her head. "Tally, that's so gross."

"You should have seen me," Tally said. "I had this stream of—"

"Okay, enough!" I begged her. "Anyway, your lips are working just fine now, Tal. No drool in sight. Next time, wear a bib. Hey, have you heard anything about this new art teacher?" Tally tended to hear things. Lots of things. Sometimes they were even true.

"New art teacher?" Tally asked. "Are we going to be drawing in health now?"

"Uh, Tal, that class ended last semester. This semester is art. Didn't the different classroom tip you off?"

Tally looked around, blinking. "I just thought they'd switched us to a new room," she said.

"And what did you think these brushes were?" I asked, laughing and pointing at a coffee can filled with paintbrushes in the center of our table.

"Decorations," Tally declared. "Ooo, y'all, now I'm psyched. Art is gonna be so much more fun than health!"

"If this new teacher ends up being at all cool, maybe we could ask them to be one of the judges for the cover artwork," Ivy said. "That would take some of the pressure off us. Even though it's all supposed to be anonymous, we don't want people taking it personally if they don't get picked."

"That might not be a bad idea," I told her. "Shelby Simpson made a point of telling me she was entering. There's someone who will definitely take it personally if she doesn't win."

"Seriously? That's weird—I thought *4 Girls* was, like, sooooo not a PQuit thing."

I laughed. "I thought so, too."

"Oh, I can see your braces!" Tally squealed, so loudly she could probably be heard in Rhode Island.

I immediately ducked my head. The room was filling up with students, and several of them were looking in my direction. And Benny Novak was coming in the door. A sack of bricks landed in my stomach with a thud. I scooted my chair around so my back faced him.

"Paulie, you can't hide from Benny forever," Ivy said quietly. "It's not that big of a school. You shouldn't have let this go on so long. You should have texted him last night."

"I know," I muttered. "It's just—why do these two things have to be happening at the same time? Not only am I freaked out because he never called me, but now I'm freaked out that he'll hate my braces. I'm getting a stomachache."

"Relax," Ivy said gently. "He just sat down near the back corner, so you won't really be in his line of vision or anything. But you've got to talk to him. I'm sure there's a really simple explanation for the Christmas thing. You're going to make yourself sick worrying about it."

"I know," I whispered.

"Why are we whispering?" Tally whispered.

"Paulina's bummed about the braces," Ivy told her.

"Oh, Paulina, are you in absolutely excruciatingly deplorable agony?" Tally whispered.

That made me laugh, even though it meant showing my teeth again. Excruciatingly deplorable agony. Tally's talent for drama seemed right on the money here.

"Yes," I said. "Absolutely. In more ways than one."

As I spoke, my eyes fell on Shelby, who had staked out a table near the door for her PQuit friends.

"Where is this mystery teacher?" Ivy asked, looking around as the second bell rang.

Just as the bell finished ringing, Miko came in. She gave the PQuits a little wave, and Shelby pulled her bag off an empty chair to make room, but much to my surprise, Miko bypassed their seats for our table.

It wasn't the first time Miko had chosen to sit with us instead of her old friends, but somehow it seemed as if people had noticed this time. Shelby stared after Miko for a moment, looking stung. Then she leaned forward and whispered something to Daphne, who shrieked with laughter.

"Hey," Miko said. "Phew—I beat the teacher. I thought I was going to be late for my first class with her. I hate making a bad first impression."

"She? Do you know who it is?" I asked.

"I was talking to Janelle on the way over, the one whose mom teaches chemistry? She told me what she knew from stuff her mom said: that the new teacher's name is Sabine Delacroix, and she's French. She's, like, an actual painter, which seems cool. Galleries sell her stuff and everything. I have to remember to check later to see if she has a website," Miko said. "She—"

Miko's voice trailed off suddenly as a woman walked briskly into the room, pulling the door closed behind her.

"Oh!" Tally whispered. "That must be her."

For some reason I had been expecting a young woman, maybe dressed in bright colors and an exotic scarf and a long ruffly skirt. That was more or less how I pictured art teachers, since both of the art teachers I'd had in elementary school had fit that general description. But this woman was more like a grandmother in age, with a lined face, bright-blue eyes, and snow-white hair in a short brush cut. She was tall and slender in simple black pants and a turtleneck, with shiny disclike earrings swinging slightly.

"Good morning, everyone," she said, speaking with a singsong accent. "I am Ms. Delacroix. I'm very happy to be joining you at Bixby. We will be working closely together this semester, and your attendance and effort will determine your grade, but I am not to just give you a grade on the art you make. My job is to help you find the creative seed already inside you and help it to grow. To tap into your full potential, even when it does not seem easy. I expect a great deal from you. Not just playing around with doodles. You will work. *Oui?* Yes?"

I nodded, feeling slightly apprehensive. If what Miko had heard was true, this woman was a professional artist. I was the furthest thing from it. I could barely draw a circle that wasn't lopsided. Art was supposed to be a stress-free class!

"Before I ask students to create their own art, I always like to share some pictures first, to see what captures your imagination. It's okay if you don't like something. Sometimes we need to know what we don't like in order to decide what we want to paint or draw, what we want to accomplish."

Ms. Delacroix pulled down the projection screen, dimmed the lights, and opened a laptop sitting on her desk.

"So, we will look at a few images by well-known artists. We begin with some paintings. First, Karl Schinkel."

The first image on the screen was of a massive, towering cathedral looming in a beautiful sky and illuminated by a setting sun. Everything looked so perfect and real and alive, I couldn't believe it was a painting.

"I show you this one to help you see that no subject, no vision is too big for an artist to take on. Never limit yourself."

We all sat in silence looking at the painting. Miko was leaning forward, her hand under her chin, her expression dreamy and thoughtful.

A new painting appeared, this one of a woman in a simple red dress in front of a window that looked out over a golden field.

"Oh, I love Hopper," Miko murmured. I glanced at her. She knew designers and classical music and now painters, too? There was so much more to her than I'd imagined when we had first met. I was starting to think she was the smartest person I knew.

"This painting is by Edward Hopper," said

Ms. Delacroix. "So much simpler, smaller scale, but so much to think about here. Who is the woman? Where is she? What is she thinking about?"

The last painting she showed us was all orange, with a roughly painted yellow rectangle in the middle, by someone named Mark Rothko. She switched on the light again.

"Rothko expresses himself not so much through a subject at all, but through pure color," Ms. Delacroix told us. "Three very different artists inspired by and expressing three very different things here. Is one of these paintings better than the others?"

Everyone began talking at once.

"Schinkel!" Shelby was saying. "Schinkel's is definitely best because it looked like it was the hardest to paint."

"No, Hopper," Tally said. "It's so emotional! It tells a story!"

"Definitely not Rothko," I heard Benny say. "Anybody could paint a yellow rectangle."

"I agree," I said, and instantly regretted it. Was Benny going to think I was trying to get back on his good side? Was he going to think I was trying to talk TO him without talking to him? I ducked my head. *Stop overthinking*, I told myself. *Just shut up*.

Ms. Delacroix let us all jabber for a minute, then raised her hand. "These are all very good points," she said. "But think about my question again. Is one of these paintings *better* than the others?"

"No," Miko said.

The teacher acknowledged Miko with a small smile. "No?" she asked. "All three are the same? And tell me your name, please."

"I'm Miko Suzuki. All three of these paintings are completely different," Miko said. "Maybe one seems stronger technically, and one seems like the artist was creating a new art form by just using color. It's like music—we like a certain kind because on some level we just get what the composer is really feeling because we feel the same thing. No one kind of music works for every single person. It's the same with art. Nobody can say one of them is better or that one of them is worse. Everyone's answer would be different, and nobody is right. We don't really even have to know why we love a certain composer or a certain painting. It's just that some kind of connection has been made between the artist and the person."

"Yes, thank you," Ms. Delacroix said, pausing for a moment with her eyes on Miko before nodding and looking around at everyone. "I would like everyone to remember what Miko has said, because this is a true thing. This is also how my class will work. Nobody in this class will be the best artist or the worst. All I require is that you work hard and that you are serious. We will talk about what interests us and why, and what we like or do not like and why. When we know what kind of art or artist moves us, we are better able to learn to be good artists ourselves. *Vous comprenez*—do you understand?"

She dimmed the lights again, and we looked at more images. We saw paintings and prints and sculptures, Egyptian artifacts and African masks and things called installations. Some of them, like the ancient masks, were fascinating. Were they art? I'd never thought about it that way. Other things, like pictures of long lightbulbs arranged in geometric patterns, I found mystifying. What made that art? And yet there it was, a famous picture hanging in a museum. Did that mean I just didn't have the ability to know something artistically great when I saw it? The thought made me uncomfortable.

Ms. Delacroix gave each person the chance, if they wanted, to talk about what they liked best and why. I decided to keep my mouth shut. I didn't want to say something stupid and have her write me off in the very first class. Plus, I didn't want to call any more attention to myself, especially from Benny.

"I really love it when an artist re-creates something by hand that looks superrealistic," Tally said. "So you look at something and you could swear it's a photograph, but somebody actually painted it. That just amazes me."

Ms. Delacroix nodded.

"Well, I feel like I just don't get some of the modern sculpture things," Shelby said. "Like the one picture of that sculpture that just looked like a smushed car. Or that one of the fluorescent lights arranged in different shapes. It sort of seems random to me, like they're doing it just to try to be edgy or something."

I hated to agree with Shelby, but I found myself nodding a little.

"I feel that, too," Daphne said. "To me, a smushed-up cube of metal is nothing compared to a painting that really represented something, like that Hopper painting of the woman in front of her window."

"I think many people feel just the same way," Ms. Delacroix said. "But this artist who does these metal sculptures is very famous. You can find his work at some of the most important museums in the world. This is the wonderful thing about the world of art—there are no boundaries. There is room for everyone."

A guy on Benny's lacrosse team named Mark raised his hand, and Ms. Delacroix pointed at him.

"What I actually think is really cool is portraits of people that were done, like, four, maybe five hundred years ago," he said. "It's like you can see a picture of some guy that's, like, from Shakespeare's time or something, but when you actually look at his face, he could be some dude you'd see on the street. Like, they're wearing these crazy things like the superhigh collars and the poofy sleeves, but when you focus in on the face, you realize how regular they look, and it's like, wow, yeah, people really did have regular lives then just like us, and maybe in five hundred more years everything about us will seem weird except for our faces."

"Your face will probably always seem weird," Benny said with a grin, and everyone laughed, including Mark. Ms. Delacroix smiled. I became fascinated with the eraser on my pencil, heat creeping into my face. Without actually looking, I couldn't tell if Benny had looked my way at all. Usually he'd shoot me a look if he cracked people up in class. *He's definitely not speaking to me*, I thought. *I knew it.* But . . . why?

"No, but I totally get what Mark is saying," Ivy said. "I feel that way about paintings of historical events, like something from the American Revolution. This stuff is so distant to us because it predates photography and video, and so we're kind of removed from the experience. It's just something we study in history class. We can't ever see those things with our own eyes. But then you see a painting done by someone who did see it with their own eyes, and suddenly it becomes much more real."

"So true," Ms. Delacroix said.

There were still hands up when the bell rang. It was pretty cool—people who had never talked in class had done so today. But I kept my hand firmly at my side. Ms. Delacroix seemed so no-nonsense. And she obviously knew a whole lot about art—real art. There was something about her I found very intimidating. If I couldn't say something smart about art, I wasn't sure I wanted to say anything at all.

"Next time, we will get our hands dirty and start making some art of our own," Ms. Delacroix promised. "But also we will see more art and have more talks like this one. *On va bien s'amuser*—that will be good!"

"That was cool," Ivy said as we walked toward our lockers. "I like how she really seemed to listen to us, you know, like what we had to say was on her level."

"I know, right?" Miko said. "She's the real deal! And we're not just going to be drawing or mushing up clay—we're really going to be learning, and looking at art and talking about it."

"I guess," I said. I had my book bag open, and I was pretending to look for something really important. What I was actually doing was creating a diversion so I could pretend not to notice Benny and Mark were coming through the door. He might have hesitated a moment, then he continued down the hall with Mark. My heart sank. *He's ignoring me*, I thought.

"And her hair is awesome," Tally said. "It's so perfectly silver white, and I love the way it sticks up like that. When I'm old I want to look like that. But I want to talk with a French accent, too—it sounds so cool."

Miko came to a sudden stop and smacked her forehead.

"Geez, I just remembered I have a French vocab quiz today. How did I manage to forget that? I cannot concentrate these days! I'm gonna have to skip lunch and study. I've got to run and grab the vocab list out of my locker, guys. See you later," she called over her shoulder.

"Miko must be feeling psyched about that class," Ivy said.

"Of all of us, Miko's the best artist," I said.

Tally wagged her finger at me. "She's not the best, *Pauliee*. She's just the artist we happen to connect with. We feel *eee*motional about her work—she *moooves* us, *oui*?" Tally said, imitating Ms. Delacroix's accent perfectly.

Ivy laughed. I tried to smile, but what I was really trying to do was not cry. Benny Novak had totally just ignored me.

"That's her exactly," Ivy said. "How do you do

that—make yourself sound exactly like somebody else?"

"Eet eez how I express myself, Ivee," Tally continued. "It is le acting. *Vous comprenez?*"

Ivy laughed.

"We need to get le going, though. We're going to be late for next period," I mumbled.

"That's right. We do not want le detention," Ivy said, starting down the hall. We walked quickly, the three of us together. Tally linked her arm through mine as we walked in perfect synchronization, our legs moving at exactly the same time.

"Le definitely not," she said.

"Paulie," Ivy said, leaning in. "What's up? Are you okay?"

I shook my head. "Le definitely not," I repeated.

"Oh, Paulie," Ivy said. "You've got to talk to the boy."

I nodded. But once again, I said nothing. Nothing at all.

· chapter ·
5

Kevin and I had just gotten off the bus that afternoon when my cell phone rang. My heart jumped. Could it be Benny? Pulling off one of my mittens as I trudged up the recently shoveled front walk, I grabbed my phone out of my pocket and answered it, my head down to fend off the icy breeze blasting down the street.

"Hey, it's me, Miko!" I heard.

I swallowed my disappointment and tried to sound cheerful. "Oh, hi! I'm just getting home. Hang on one second while I open my front door so my hand doesn't freeze."

"Paulie, I'm going to break the ice on all these puddles before I go inside. Paulie, did you hear me?" Kevin called.

He was already making his way up our sidewalk and smashing his heel down on all the ice he could find.

"Yes, I heard you. I'm on the phone, and I'm going

in. It's freezing out here," I told my little brother.

The minute I was inside my house I went and stood over the heating grate in the front hall, pressing the cell phone to my ear.

"Hey, Meek, I'm back. What's up?"

"So yeah, I ended up running into Ms. Delacroix after school, and we had this really great talk. She showed me some of her paintings that are up on her website. She is just phenomenal. And we got to talking about school and art, and I told her all about *4 Girls* and showed her the cover art I created for that first issue. And guess what—she said she thought it was as professional a piece as she'd ever seen! She said the idea of drawing different girls swinging from the stars was really original, and that my use of color was really innovative, and that I was good at drawing faces and hands, which apparently a lot of people aren't. She loved it!"

"Wow, Miko, that is so great!" I told my friend.

"I know, right?" Miko said. "She was really interested in *4 Girls,* and she had tons of questions, especially when I told her our current issue was a collaboration with other students. Apparently she used to be an editorial director of this French art journal when she lived in Paris. In a way, it was kind of like what we're doing with *4 Girls.* Isn't that an amazing coincidence?"

"It is," I said, kicking off my shoes so I could stand on the grate and feel the heat directly on my feet. Of course Ms. Delacroix had worked at a real art magazine. That just figured.

"Oh, Paulina, she is so cool. We talked about painting and drawing, and she told me how she and her family lived in Paris when she was my age, and she used to go to the museums and see the famous paintings. I could have talked to her all day, but my dad had come to pick me up for one of my extra violin lessons, and I kind of lost track of the time. He sent me this pretty irritated text, so I had to run off."

"What a bummer," I said. "But it sounds like you had a good talk."

"Oh, we really did," Miko said. "I think we could actually be sort of friends, I mean, as much as you can with a teacher. Anyway, the reason I was calling is I had this idea. What if we asked Ms. Delacroix to be our faculty adviser for *4 Girls*?"

"Faculty adviser?" I asked. "Do we, uh, need one of those? I'm not even sure what they do."

"A faculty adviser would give us advice, some guidance," Miko said. "I just think it would be really cool if she said yes. I mean, not only is she a real artist, but she's edited an art journal herself. It could be really amazing for us!"

It seemed to me that *4 Girls* was doing just fine on

its own, without an adviser. It kind of sounded like we'd be making more work for ourselves, not less. But Miko sounded so excited, I didn't want to just shoot the idea down. Was it such a bad thing to be pushed to be a little more professional? *Yes*, a tiny voice said inside my head.

"Well," I said, "as soon as I've gotten warmed up and had a cup of hot chai, I'll give Ivy a call and ask her what she thinks about it."

"Oh, that would be—"

Miko's voice broke off suddenly. "Hello? Miko, are you there?" I thought maybe my phone had dropped the call.

"I will," I heard Miko's voice say, slightly muffled as if she had her hand over the phone. "I am, Dad, I just—okay. Okay!"

I waited silently, feeling like I was eavesdropping on half of a private conversation.

"Hey, sorry about that. I have to go right now or my father is going to have a meltdown," Miko said. "I'm supposed to be doing these music-theory workbooks he got. Talk to you later, okay? Bye!"

"Bye!" I said, a moment too late, because Miko had already hung up.

I walked to the kitchen, unzipping my coat along the way, and put the kettle on the stove. Miko had sounded so animated and excited before her father came to scold her for being on the phone. I couldn't imagine having my mom do something like that.

Of the four of us, Miko was definitely the one under the most pressure. With her audition coming up soon, things were only going to get more intense. There were mornings she showed up at school looking so tired I wondered if she'd even slept. I really liked Miko, and I worried about her sometimes. I didn't like to see my friend so stressed out.

I thought about asking the new art teacher to be our adviser. The more I thought about it, the more the idea worried me. We did things in our own way, working around people's schedules. We didn't really have an official process or even a set schedule for publishing *4 Girls*—somehow it just got done. If one of us dropped the ball on something, someone else picked it up. What if a faculty adviser wanted to change all that? Especially one who had already announced she expected us to be professional in class. As the wind rattled the windows, I pulled the box of chai tea bags down from the shelf, stood close to the stove where the kettle was chugging away on the front burner, and called Ivy on my cell.

"Hiya," I said when she answered. "So Miko just called all excited because she ran into Ms. Delacroix, and they had this great talk about art and everything. Miko showed her the cover she made for the first issue of *4 Girls,* and I guess she really liked it."

"Cool," Ivy said. "Glad to see our Miko being appreciated."

"Yeah, you should have heard her. They talked about Paris and museums and all that, and apparently she used to edit an art journal there or something. Miko was so impressed that she thinks we should ask Ms. Delacroix if she'll be our faculty adviser."

"Faculty adviser?" Ivy asked. "Who says we need one of those? Is this a new requirement from Principal Finley?"

I sighed, placing a tea bag into my mug and watching a jet of steam come from the teakettle.

"No, there's no requirement. This is just Miko's idea. I guess she thinks because Ms. Delacroix is a professional artist and editor that she'd somehow be helpful."

"I sort of feel like we're doing fine right now," Ivy told me. "Why try and fix something that isn't broken? We don't need an adviser."

"No, you're right. I don't think we need one, either. But the thing is, Miko seems to really want this. Her judgment is usually pretty good."

"Well, yeah," Ivy said as my teakettle began to whistle. "But she's basing all this on exactly one class and one conversation. She doesn't really know this teacher all that well. And we have no idea what she'd be like to work with. We've had total control over the content and the schedule of *4 Girls* from the beginning. We've done things our way, in our own time, and it's worked out. What if she wants to mess with all that? What if she wants to make it more rigid or something? It's not like we can ask someone to advise our club, then fire them if we don't like their input."

"I totally see your point," I said, pouring the steaming hot water into my mug. "And actually, I agree. It's just . . . Ivy, Miko seemed so sure that this would be a good thing for us. You should have heard her just now, that is, until her father started yelling in the background for her to get off the phone. And hey, we don't even know if Ms. Delacroix would accept. I'd hate to just reject the idea totally, when it's obviously so important to Miko. Because Miko is important to us!"

"Well, what if we wait, take some time to get to know Ms. Delacroix better, and see how she operates day-to-day in class," Ivy suggested.

I blew on my mug of chai, which smelled delicious as it steeped.

"I guess we could do it that way," I said. "But I think Miko had the Collaboration Concepts issue in mind. She's under so much pressure because of this Music Conservatory audition, and it's only going to get worse the closer it gets. Plus, who even knows how long Ms. Delacroix is staying? I had two different art teachers in two years in elementary school. They don't always stick around."

My mother walked into the kitchen, blew me a kiss, and pulled a plate out of the refrigerator.

"Organic cheese-cube snacks," she whispered, and I nodded and smiled as she placed the plate on the table. I would eat a few when I got off the phone, just to make her happy, but really I craved Cheetos.

"True," Ivy replied. "And Miko does have good judgment on this stuff. I mean, it could end up being a really good thing. I just feel like it might be a bad idea to get us roped into something when we don't know how it will end up working."

I sighed, tried to take a sip of my chai, and put the mug back down when I found it was still too hot to drink. My mother was unwrapping a frozen casserole and preheating the oven. I hoped it was something good. The cold weather made me feel constantly starving. I wanted comfort food. Mashed potatoes. Lasagna. Sausages.

"Okay, what if we do this," I began. "The whole theme of this issue is collaboration. We've been focusing on collaboration between us and the students, but what if we extend the concept to include faculty? We could ask Ms. Delacroix to be our adviser for this one specific issue. It works with the theme, plus we were talking about having a faculty judge for the competition, remember? So if we end up having a great experience, we could ask her to become our official adviser. If it ends up creating more work or we don't all get along or whatever, then after this we just go back to the way things were."

There was a brief silence. I tried my chai again. It was still hot, but ready to drink. It tasted delicious.

"Paulina, you may have a future as an ambassador," Ivy said. "That is a brilliant idea."

"Cool!" I said. "Miko will be so psyched. Though I guess we should check with Tally, too, to make sure it's okay with her."

"You know Tally, she's usually on board with just about anything. But I'll shoot her a text," Ivy said. "And I'll let you know when I hear back."

"Perfect!" I said. "Then I can call Miko. Actually, I probably shouldn't call her. I don't want her to get in any more trouble. I'll e-mail her. I'm sure she'll want to be the one to ask Ms. Delacroix."

"Coolio," Ivy said.

The front door slammed, I heard a dull thud, then Kevin shot into the kitchen, almost colliding with my mother.

"Kevin, my goodness," she exclaimed. "You could have knocked me down."

"I have frostbite!" he yelled, holding his hands out. "I just saw Luke Zimmerman, and he said at least two of my fingers will probably fall off!"

"Is that Kevin I hear? What's going on?" Ivy asked.

"Apparently he has frostbite," I told Ivy as my mother took both of Kevin's hands in her own and rubbed them briskly. "He'll probably die."

Kevin stuck his tongue out at me.

"Well, tell him I enjoyed knowing him," Ivy said. "So listen, do you want to talk about today? About Benny?"

I turned to face the cabinets and lowered my voice. "I totally, totally do," I said. "But I can't right now. Can we talk tonight? I'll be in my room later doing homework."

"Definitely," Ivy said. "Call me when you have some privacy."

"I will," I said, relieved. "Thanks—bye."

I put my phone onto the counter. "Ivy says if you end up dying of frostbite, she enjoyed knowing you."

"I'm not going to die," Kevin said, rolling his eyes. "You don't die of having your fingers drop off."

"How about we get a little hot chocolate into you, Kev," my mother said, putting the kettle back on the burner. "Just to make sure you get warmed up, and you get to keep all ten of your fingers. Toes too."

"Can I have whipped cream?" Kevin asked.

"We never even have whipped cream, Kev," I told him.

"No, we do! Left over from when we had pumpkin pie at Christmas!" Kevin insisted. "I want a huge squirt of it on top. Okay, Mom?"

The kettle, which was still hot, had already begun to whistle.

"I think that can be arranged," my mother said with a smile as she took down a package of hot chocolate and poured it into Kevin's favorite mug.

"But it would be really cool to have a finger fall off," Kevin said. "Especially if it happened at school! In the cafeteria! I could send my food back, and they'd find a finger in it! Wouldn't that be hilarious?"

My mind was back on Benny and on how long I would have to wait before I could call Ivy to discuss my theory that Benny had totally ignored me after art class. But suddenly what Kevin had just said appeared as a picture in my mind. I entertained a brief vision of Shelby Simpson finding a finger sticking out of her chicken chow mein, and I smiled.

"You know, Kev," I said. "I think you're right. That would be hilarious."

· chapter ·
6

Ivy and I sat at the desk in the empty office the school let us use as our *4 Girls* headquarters. Though Miko had already asked Ms. Delacroix to be our adviser, the teacher had asked to meet with us all so that we could "decide" if we really wanted her to do the job. *Professional indeed*, I thought with a sigh. Unfortunately, Miko's ever-more-complicated schedule left her no time to come to the meeting herself, leaving me and Ivy waiting for Tally to show up with Ms. Delacroix. I tapped my pencil nervously on the desk and checked the time.

"Okay, how's this?" Ivy asked.

On the computer, she had pulled up her competition announcement and added:

Blogpost: Calling All Artists!
Posted by: 4Girls

Great news, readers and contributors! Our new art teacher, Ms. Delacroix, has agreed to be a special guest judge for the cover submissions. Remember, the deadline is January 14. Multiple submissions from the same person are definitely permitted. And tell your friends!!!

"As soon as it's official with Ms. Delacroix, I'll post it," Ivy said.

"Looks perfect," I told her. "I'm so glad you know how to do all this stuff."

I was embarrassed that I had so little computer savvy. Here was another area where Ms. Delacroix might definitely judge my "professional" abilities lacking. I could get into our blog to read and respond to posts, but I still found the process of creating new content or banners really confusing. I lived in terror of accidentally pushing a button and doing something terrible like deleting all the submissions while simultaneously turning on the webcam to record and broadcast me as I muttered to myself while doing homework.

"Oh, you'll figure it out eventually. Hey, look, we already have a submission," Ivy said, pointing at a counter she'd created at the top of the page. "So when you're checking in to see what's there, just input your administrator code, then you just click on the counter, and that takes you to the slide show of art."

"But this isn't visible to everyone checking the blog, is it?" I asked.

Ivy shook her head. "Nope, just to us. That's what the administrator code is for. We don't want people to feel like they're going to be judged by the whole school if they send something in."

"Definitely not," I said. Like we didn't have enough judging going on just by being in school. Like people probably hadn't noticed by now that Benny and I weren't speaking and were wondering why! I sighed, trying to chase the thought from my mind. I could not get weepy when we were about to meet with a teacher for a professional meeting.

"What time is it?" I asked, turning to look at the wall clock. "I hope Tally didn't get the time or place mixed up or something. Maybe one of us should have gone to get Ms. Delacroix instead."

"Yeah, but Tally had class right next to the art room last period," Ivy said. "She'll figure it out—they'll get here. I'm still confused about what's going on with Miko, though. Why can't she be here?"

"She's making up an English exam," I explained.

"But the English exam isn't for two days, is it?" Ivy asked.

"No, it isn't, but Miko has to leave school early that day to get some kind of superpowered coaching for her audition. Has she told you about that part? The Music Conservatory thing isn't the kind of audition where you just get up and play a piece. It's a two-day audition. On the first day, you have to go through this whole exam on music theory, whatever that is. I'm not quite clear on that yet."

"Wow," Ivy said. "I guess I didn't realize the audition was two days long."

"Yeah, it is," I said. "Monday the fifteenth and Tuesday the sixteenth. Miko's really got her work cut out for her. And I'm sure it will just get more intense the closer the audition gets."

The hallway outside the office was suddenly filled with the sound of Tally's bubbly voice.

"Good, there they are now," Ivy said.

I opened a notebook, feeling like I should look official or something for our first *4 Girls* meeting with Ms. Delacroix. I wanted to like the teacher as much as Miko did and feel as comfortable around her as Tally seemed to, but the woman just flat-out made me nervous. In the classroom I was just one of a whole bunch of students—I could just keep my mouth shut and not say anything. But this was one-on-one. Ms. Delacroix was a real artist and had edited a magazine and was European and sophisticated. I couldn't help but worry that she'd realize I wasn't as gifted as Miko or as savvy as Ivy or as perpetually interesting as Tally. That where those things were concerned, I was kind of faking my way along.

"And my sister kept saying really loudly how stupid she thought the painting was and that it looked like a kindergartner had done it, and finally she turns to this guy who's standing next to her, and she says, 'Seriously, you or I could paint something better than this, don't you think?' and it turns out the guy is the painter! And she's been standing there saying all these terrible things about his work right in front of him!"

Tally and Ms. Delacroix came through the door with Tally still talking a mile a minute.

"My sister was absolutely mortified. She almost dropped dead right on the spot! To this day she refuses to go to any part of a museum that has works by living artists, because she's so afraid it will happen again."

"Tally has been entertaining me," Ms. Delacroix said, turning to me and Ivy with a smile. "I hope we haven't kept you waiting."

"Not at all," Ivy said. "Paulina and I were just checking the blog. Miko showed you the address, right?"

"She did, yes, that is clever," Ms. Delacroix said.

"And she gave me copies of your first issue to take home and showed me how to access the online issue you made when you were in New York. Three days at *City Nation*, this is something. What a wonderful experience for you."

"Oh, you have no idea," Tally said. "The people, the drama! Disappearing movie stars and terrifying editors and sneaky interns and forbidden colors. I have never seen a crazier bunch of people in one room, and that includes Drama Club. I loved every minute of it."

"And they loved every minute of you," Ivy told her. "But we should get this meeting started."

"Yes," Ms. Delacroix agreed. "I'm happy that Miko has asked me to be your adviser, but I want to know what you think, too."

"Oh, Miko's always right about these things," Tally said breezily. "If she thinks you should be our adviser, then I think so, too."

Whoa there, Tal, I thought. *Slow down.*

Ms. Delacroix laughed. "Ah, but you have no way to know that I will not turn into one of these terrifying people like you saw at *City Nation*, Tally. Let us talk about it a little bit. You have questions, I am sure."

"Well, I was wondering how it would work," Ivy said. "If you're our adviser, what kind of commitment are we making to each other and what kinds of things do you see happening?"

Good job, Ivy, I thought with relief. I didn't want to be the one to ask, because I was afraid it might come out wrong or that Ms. Delacroix would take it personally. *Stop second-guessing and follow Ivy's lead*, I told myself. This meeting was Ms. Delacroix's idea, after all.

"Right," I said, "and also, will it change the way we work? The scheduling and who does what? Because we're not all that structured about it."

Ms. Delacroix nodded. "Good questions, yes," she said. "Miko specifically mentioned my giving advice and suggestions, which I would like to do, but with the understanding that they are just that—suggestions. *4 Girls* is your magazine, made by you. You have the final say. I would like to meet with all of you several times so you can share with me how things are coming along, what is still missing, what problems might have come up. And if you agree I should be one of the judges for the cover submissions, then I would like to put aside a time and place for all of us to do that together. But again, I am only making a vote and sharing my own thoughts on what is submitted. Beyond that, I can perhaps offer some access to materials and computer programs you may find helpful. I have a very good computer in my studio at home. And because I am a faculty member, I am responsible always for making sure no school rules or policies are being broken. That means anywhere—in my classroom or out. I don't imagine this is any real issue for *4 Girls*, but I do have to say that up front. If I bring some violation of rules to your attention, and it is not fixed, I would have no choice but to share that with the principal. That is the downside, I think, because you have not had that kind of supervision before."

I remembered the drama that had gone along with our first issue—when an anonymous blogpost accused the four of us of cheating and breaking school rules. The four of us had decided together to go to Principal Finley and tell her about the accusation, which was completely untrue. *It would have seemed different*, I thought, *scarier, to have a teacher looking over our shoulders in the middle of all that, when we wanted to deal with the problem ourselves.*

"That makes sense to me," Ivy said. "So you're saying that other than that, this can be pretty much whatever we want to make it—that we're not establishing any new rules here."

Ms. Delacroix nodded. "Yes. And I think also if you decide you work better without an adviser, you should be free to say so. We will not, as they say, carve anything in stone."

Ivy's eyes met mine. She probably knew me well enough to guess I was still a little hesitant.

If I don't speak up, Ivy's going to hold off, I thought. *Come on, Paulina, make the leap. This isn't brain surgery, it's just a faculty adviser!*

"I think it sounds good," I said.

"I do too," Ivy said immediately.

"I did," Tally said. "I mean, I will. I still do. I never didn't. Oh, that's wrong, that's one of those twice noes. I'm always getting that wrong in English class."

"I have difficulty with that myself sometimes, Tally. Your English is a complicated language. But I am glad you are all agreeing," Ms. Delacroix said.

"Great. I think it just became official!" Ivy said. "Welcome to *4 Girls*."

"Ah, thank you," Ms. Delacroix said. "I am pleased. I like what you are doing here. I think it is both good and important. It is never too soon to start taking yourselves seriously as artists."

I wasn't sure I did take myself seriously as an artist. I took Miko seriously as one, though.

"Ivy, maybe you should show Ms. Delacroix the administrator-code thing and how to get into the submissions page," I said.

"Good idea," Ivy said, turning to look at the computer screen. Ms. Delacroix pulled her chair closer to Ivy's to get a better look at the screen.

"Okay, so if you go to the main page on the blog, you click up here where it says 'Site Admins,' and it will ask you to input an administrator code. The code is 4Girls7777. We made it that because we're four seventh-graders, if that helps you remember it. That gives you access to any submissions that have been made and gives you moderator status on the blog, so you have the ability to go in and add text or remove a posting if it's inappropriate for some reason. Our rules are basically no names, no name-calling, no gossiping, no flame wars, that kind of thing."

Ms. Delacroix pulled her chair a little closer to the computer. She was wearing a dark-gray sweater dress today, and long, skinny earrings of silver and turquoise. She put on a pair of simple black-rimmed glasses.

"Ah, now I see better. It is good that I can look, but I think I will not speak up or contribute on the blog," she said. "This should have the feel of a no-teacher place, don't you think?"

Phew, I thought. *I'm glad she said it first so one of us didn't have to.*

"I think so, too," I said. "And Ivy, can you go to the page where the cover submissions are?"

"Yes. You just go back to the previous page and click here on 'Cover Submissions,'" Ivy explained. "So here's the first submission that went up. If you roll the cursor over the top corner of the image, it shows you the date and time of the posting."

"Hmmm," Ms. Delacroix said, looking at the image.

The artist had used something like Photoshop and created some additional art to make the picture of a child's green balloon floating in the air with a long string dangling beneath it. The bottom of the balloon looked normal, but the top had been modified to look like a grassy plain, and there were tiny giraffes and zebras grazing on it. At the very bottom of the long string, a monkey was hanging on and waving. I thought it was cute and inventive.

"So you have not placed any limits on the kind of work that is acceptable?" Ms. Delacroix asked.

Uh-oh, I thought. That didn't sound good.

"What kind of limits?" Ivy asked.

"Defining what is and is not considered original art," she replied. "This piece, for example, is using someone else's photographs, at least we presume they are, and the artist's work here has been in using a program to cut and paste them together."

"You mean this isn't art?" Tally asked, looking confused.

"Oh no, Tally, certainly that isn't what I mean to say," Ms. Delacroix replied. "That is a different discussion, and one that doesn't really have clear answers. If you place some limits on what you will accept, say drawings and paintings, photographs perhaps, it becomes a more challenging competition. More professional."

Oh no, I thought. *Here we go. It hasn't been more than ten minutes and we're unprofessional?*

"But that's what we didn't want," I blurted. I almost smacked my forehead because I made it sound like we weren't serious about the cover, and we *were*. I was nervous and speaking without thinking clearly. "What I mean," I said more slowly, "is the whole theme of this issue is Collaboration Concepts. We're trying to reach out to everybody, not just the people who feel like their work is good enough to be published or something. *4 Girls* has ended up being sort of a showcase for how different all of us are from one another and how that's a really good thing, actually. I think it's one of the things that makes *4 Girls* special—very different people working together to create something. The whole collaboration idea is to try and kind of make that happen on a bigger level with our readers."

"Ah," Ms. Delacroix said, nodding. "I see."

Did she? I wasn't completely convinced.

"But you all have to decide in the end what the limits are," she added. "And when something ceases to feel like something creative and begins more to feel like someone else's work is being borrowed," Ms. Delacroix added. I shot Ivy a quick look. Was that what she was saying, then?

"Okay, we'll keep that in mind," Ivy said.

"Very good," Ms. Delacroix said. "I look forward to being able to work with you. I think we are, as you say, on the same page."

I wasn't so sure about that. Whatever page Ms. Delacroix was on seemed like it was at least a chapter away from the page I was on.

But this would make Miko happy, and it didn't have to be a permanent thing. If it didn't work out, we'd go back to the way things had been before. And if it did work out, all the better for us.

If it did work out.

And to me, that was a pretty big *if*.

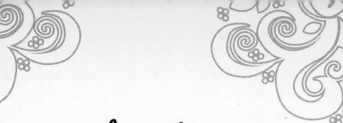

· chapter ·

7

I took off my glove and rang the doorbell nervously. What if Miko's dad answered? Was he going to be mad?

Relax, I told myself, slipping my already-freezing hand back into the glove. Miko needed a copy of *Animal Farm* so she could start her extra-credit reading, and I happened to have a copy. *I'm just bringing it over like she asked*, I told myself.

Still, when the door opened and Miko herself was standing there and not her dad, I felt a rush of relief.

"Did you bring the book?" she asked. "Thank you so much, Paulie. I can get it back to you before they even assign it, but I need to get a head start on things where I can. If I can get most of *Animal Farm* read tonight, I'll be able to cross that off my list, at least."

She looks seriously tired, I thought, examining my

friend's pale face and the shadows under her eyes. As a blast of frigid air hit her face, her cheeks reddened suddenly.

"No worries," I said. "When they officially assign it, they'll just hand us our school copies, anyway. This is an old paperback my mom already had at home. No rush getting it back."

"I'll take good care of it," Miko said. "Brrr, it's even colder out than yesterday," she added, looking over my shoulder. "Why don't you come in for a second?"

I WAS cold. More importantly, I really wanted to talk to Miko and get a sense of how she was actually doing.

"My dad's not home right now," Miko said. "He's at the downtown office on Friday afternoons, and he doesn't get home until six usually. It's okay. I could really use a little break. My head is pounding right now."

"Okay, I will come in for a little while," I said, relieved. I followed Miko inside. She led me down a short corridor with polished, wide-planked wooden floors. I suddenly worried that I was tracking snow in, but I hadn't noticed a mat anywhere.

"This is the kitchen," Miko said, entering the room at the end of the hallway. "Pull up a chair. I'm just gonna run and tell my mom you're here for a bit."

Miko hastily filled a teakettle with water, put it on the stove to boil, then opened a door in the corner of the kitchen to reveal a tiny back staircase, which she ran up.

I sat down at the table and looked around. Miko's kitchen was much smaller than mine and extremely tidy. The stove gleamed, and the countertops were free of clutter except for a set of aluminum storage containers arranged in size order. A large clock over the sink told me in no uncertain terms it was 5:15. The house seemed totally quiet except for the ticking of the clock.

I heard creaking on the stairs, and Miko came through the door.

"Mom's on the phone," Miko said. "She'll come say hi when she's free. So does hot cocoa sound good to you?"

"You have no idea," I said. "I'd love one."

"Me too," she said.

She opened one of the overhead cabinets, took down two mugs, and retrieved a tin of cocoa from another shelf.

"Wow, I've never seen that brand before," I said, admiring the gold tin.

Miko smiled. "It's Godiva," she told me. "It is crazy good, you won't believe it. That pianist who was here on New Year's Eve brought it as a gift. I could eat it by the spoonful right out of the box."

"I can't wait to try it," I told her, my mouth watering a little. "So the assembly you missed this afternoon was pretty boring. A guy talking about the power of numbers and why being an accountant is actually, like, this incredibly exciting job. A few people that shall remain nameless actually dozed off. I'm not sure, but I think one of the eighth-grade boys might have been talking in his sleep. He kept saying something like, 'I don't have any barnacles!'"

Miko laughed. "Can't say I'm sorry I missed it," she said. "My dad got Principal Finley to agree to let me out early, since my only class after the assembly was gym. Got in an extra hour of practicing already, so hopefully he'll be happy."

Are you happy? I wanted to ask. But I decided to wait. Miko was hard to read sometimes. She could be open about her feelings, or if you pushed at the wrong time, she could close up like a clam. On the stove top, the kettle began to whistle.

"Love that sound," I said. "My stomach is already growling."

Miko carefully measured two tablespoons of the Godiva chocolate into each mug. "See this, it's actually more like chocolate shavings than powder," she pointed out. "This stuff is ridiculously fabulous."

She opened the fridge and got out a carton of milk,

which she poured into a Pyrex cup. She put that in the microwave to heat. When the bell rang a minute later, Miko poured some of the steaming milk into each mug. She frowned slightly while pouring, and I noticed again the dark circles under her eyes.

"It's much better if you make it with half water, half milk," Miko explained as she poured in the water. "Okay—it's all ready. Do you want to take these upstairs to my room?"

"If that's okay," I said. "I'm meeting Ivy for a slice at the pizza place at six, which is just, like, a five-minute walk from here, so that's perfect."

I had never been to Miko's house before. She had texted me after school asking if I had a copy of *Animal Farm*, and when I replied that I did, she asked me to drop it off at her house. I'd been excited to see her house and have a couple minutes to talk to her alone, but I hadn't thought she'd be inviting me in.

I followed Miko up the little staircase, which had smaller-than-normal steps and which wound around in a spiral. I held my cocoa carefully out in front of me. It smelled amazing, and I didn't want to spill any.

The stairway opened onto a small landing. At one end was a small bedroom and bathroom, and a narrow hallway extended to the left.

"This is my room," Miko said, leading me through the door at the end of the landing.

My first thought as I followed Miko through the door was *This is tiny!* Her room was about a third the size of mine, and *mine* wasn't exactly enormous. But everything was set up very carefully with an eye for saving space. On the left was a raised bed, like the top of a bunk bed without the bottom, built into the wall. Below that was a desk with small bookshelves on either side. The walls were decorated with prints of paintings and with black-and-white photographs of people playing the violin, some of which looked very old. Shelves were built up high on the walls, holding sweaters and hats. In the corner of the room was a music stand, and Miko's violin sat on the floor next to it, in an open case with a red velvet lining. Above that hung an open Japanese parasol painted with tiny pink flowers and a snowcapped mountain.

"Oh, I love your room, Miko. It's so you!"

"Not much space to move around," she said. "But my dad designed all this himself. He grew up in Tokyo, and a lot of the apartments there are absolutely teeny. There's all kinds of ways to make a room feel bigger."

"I'd love to sleep on a top bunk like that," I said.

"Yeah, I love it," Miko said. "It's like my own personal indoor tree house. Here, grab that chair," she told me as she climbed a few rungs up the ladder to the bed and retrieved a large decorative pillow that she tossed onto the floor.

"But where are you going to sit?" I asked.

Miko put her cocoa carefully on the floor, then flopped down on top of the pillow.

"Right here," she said. She picked up her mug, blew on it, then took a small sip.

"Ah," she said. "That is exactly what I needed. A little chocolate and a break."

I took a sip of mine, too, and almost squealed at the rich, velvety chocolate taste. "How can I ever drink plain old Swiss Miss again?" I asked.

Miko smiled briefly, then the little worried crease between her eyes appeared again.

"Meek, how *are* you doing? I mean, really? I'm a little worried about you—you look so tired."

Miko took another sip of cocoa, then placed the mug on the floor. She seemed to be deciding what to say for a moment. I waited patiently, knowing not to push.

"I have to admit, this is about as stressed out as I've ever been," she said. "I'm feeling okay about the piece I'm going to be playing for the audition. I've had so many extra violin lessons, and I must have played the thing a thousand times right here in this room. It's the music-theory part that's really tough."

"I don't really understand what music theory is," I told Miko.

"Well, it's complicated. It's basically all the stuff the music is made up of—keys, scales, chords, tempo, all sorts of things like that. The conservatory is like any superserious music program—they want students who aren't just performers but can show that they know what it is they're playing and why. Like, here's an example."

She picked up her violin from its case, and without getting up, she played a simple tune. I knew it immediately and hummed along.

"Yeah, everyone knows that from *The Sound of Music*, right?" Miko asked. "*Do, a deer, a female deer. Re, a drop of golden sun* . . . those are just different names for notes. Do is C, re is D, mi is E, and so on. All that song is really about is a basic C scale. Listen."

She played eight notes, and I sang along with the song I knew so well from watching Maria and the von Trapp children sing it dozens of times.

Miko pointed her bow at me. "Perfect. You just sang a C scale in the key of C major. That's music theory, on about the simplest level it gets. No sharps or flats, all whole notes with the same interval between each note. Easy. But then you have something like this."

She played another scale.

"Sounds the same, right?" she said. "But in this key, you have seven sharps. That's a half tone above the regular note. So at this audition, they might ask me to take something in the key of C and change it to C-sharp major, or they might ask me to play a certain chord or interval in that key, or ask me what the relative minor is to that key, which all sounds like nonsense to you, I know. But I have to know all this stuff. Not just how to play it, but I have to listen to them play things and then identify them."

"Why?" I asked.

"Well, for starters, they want to know if I have perfect pitch. You don't have to have it, and you can't really learn it. I think you're either born with it or you aren't. So if I have perfect pitch, someone can say, 'Miko, give me an F sharp,' and I play the note. Then they'll play an F sharp to see if I got it right."

Miko played one note on the violin.

"Or they might do it the other way around—they play a note and ask me what it is. If I have perfect pitch, I can identify it all by itself. Then they might do something like play a passage, and I have to tell them what key and time signature it's in. And there are all these weird intervals between notes, things like minor thirds or diminished fifths. They'll ask me to play those, or they'll play them for me and want me to tell them what key and what interval it is."

"Whoa," I said. "I'm already confused."

"That's not even the half of it," she said. "I'll play my prepared piece for them, but then they'll test my sight reading. Sight reading is basically the ability to be handed music you've never seen before and play it the first time through correctly. And there are some keys it's superhard to read in—like that one I played you that has seven sharps. So I have to practice my scales obsessively, and some of them are really hard for me."

I shook my head in amazement. "I had no idea there was so much to this, Miko. It seems crazy!"

"It's pretty standard for a school like the Music Conservatory," Miko told me, putting her violin back in its case. "That's why it's so supercompetitive to get in. That's why my dad is riding me so hard."

"About your dad . . ." I said, hesitating.

Miko gazed at me evenly with clear brown eyes. "You can ask. I'm not going to be offended or anything," she said.

"Okay . . . I just wonder . . . the violin, the whole Music Conservatory program—how much of that came from your dad, and how much is really what you want?"

There. I'd finally just asked. Miko's expression didn't change, and she didn't seem upset or irritated by the question.

"You'd think I would have a clear-cut answer to that," Miko said. "But I'm not sure I do. Starting violin lessons was my idea—that I remember. When I was around eight or something, my mother suggested I think about taking up an instrument. She and my dad both have musicians in their families. I knew right away I wanted to try the violin. And after the first year or so, my teacher told my parents I had a real gift for it, and I was already way ahead of some of her intermediate students. I guess that's when my dad first started getting kind of bossy about it. He found this new teacher for me who's taught some really gifted musicians and convinced her to take me on. And from then on, my violin was always this superserious topic for him, you know. He wanted to see that I was working really hard on it and being absolutely the best I could be. That's just his personality. He's that way about my grades, too, and I'm an only child, so that all falls on me."

"And what about your love of art?" I asked. "And design? Does he want you to be the absolute best artist, too?"

Miko shook her head. "No. In fact, he seems to see anything art related, which includes 4 Girls, as a kind of threat to my violin and my grades. Which is weird to me, because they're both creative things, right?"

I nodded.

"I don't know. I really didn't start getting interested in drawing and designing until last year, and working on *4 Girls* really brought it out in me. I mean, I surprised myself, I have to say. I didn't know creating art would be something that I would enjoy so much, and that I'd be kind of good at it. And design, like fashion design—the stuff that I got to do with Garamond when we had the *City Nation* trip—that was really great, too, but . . . I think really it's more like a hobby, you know? Something I just happen to be interested in. My dad was basically saying absolutely not about the summer design internship Garamond offered me from the first moment I mentioned it. That was actually okay. Don't get me wrong, I would have loved to do it. But I didn't feel like it was this huge thing I desperately wanted that he was keeping me from."

"But you do sort of feel that way about art?" I pressed.

Miko sighed, reaching her hand toward the open violin case and absentmindedly plucking a few of the strings.

"I might. I'm just not sure yet," she said. "Like I told you, I only really started getting interested in it recently. But the idea of being an artist, and of making a career out of painting and maybe teaching art in some way like Ms. Delacroix does . . . I think about that a lot. I can see myself living that life. It just feels so *me*, you know? The thing that really bugs me, Paulie, is it's like my parents want me to decide right now or something. The conservatory would be a big deal, but it's only a summer program. From there my dad sees me applying to be a student there full time in high school, which would require a scholarship that I don't even want to think about, to pave the way to get into a top music college like Juilliard. This is what he keeps pressing on me—that if I want that, I have to work my butt off now and get into this summer program. But what if that isn't what I want? What if I would rather be an artist? He never actually asks me that—he just assumes music is the way to go. I'm thirteen years old—am I really supposed to know without a doubt who I want to be yet? It doesn't seem fair that I have to pick one or the other now."

"It isn't fair," I said firmly. "And whatever your dad thinks, I don't think you do have to decide right now. I mean, let's say you do get into the Music Conservatory—that's going to make your summer mostly about music. But that doesn't mean your whole future is decided. Maybe you could look at it as just being a possibility. You've got all these options opening up. Miko, really, you're so good at so many things. You shouldn't have to choose just one. You've got, what, ten more days till the audition, right?"

Miko nodded.

"Okay, so after that, a big part of the pressure right now will be off. That part of things will be out of your hands. We'll be finishing up the issue around then, but soon we'll start working on the next one, and you'll be right back in there doing it with us. And you've got the whole rest of the semester in Ms. Delacroix's art class, so you will get to be working on art, for school! Just try to hang in there. And as far as your dad goes, maybe every once in a while make it clear what you want. There's nothing wrong with taking a stand sometimes, if you've thought it through and it's something important to you."

Miko's eyes grew shiny with tears. She got up and gave me a quick, tight hug.

"Thank you," she said. "The way you put it makes total sense. It's so clear. I've been thinking and thinking and thinking about all this, but I never come out of it with anything that helps. What you just said—that's exactly what I needed to hear. What I need to remember. And I *do* need to take a stand. Thanks, Paulie."

I flushed slightly, feeling wonderful. "Well, my mother IS a shrink," I said. "Some of it probably rubbed off."

"So listen, what's going on with you?" Miko asked. "I know I've basically been living under a rock recently, but what's the deal with Benny? Don't think I haven't noticed how bummed you've been."

I groaned. "Oh, it's such a mess now," I said. "I should have just said something to him the first day we were back at school. I've let it go way too long."

"So the last thing you heard was when he was sick over break and he was going to bring you a Christmas present when he felt better?" Miko asked.

I nodded.

"Yep. He never called after that. I have no idea why. And when I saw him in school the first day, he seemed . . . I don't know—uncomfortable. Like something wasn't right. I should have just asked him or sent him a text that day—that's what Ivy kept telling me to do. Not saying anything just makes it worse every day that goes by. I mean, I figure there's a problem. Probably he doesn't want to go out anymore, maybe he likes someone else now, or maybe it's just me. I mean, that much is obvious, right?"

"Um, *no*, it isn't obvious. Why would you jump to that conclusion? Paulie, no offense, but I think you're making a big mistake here," Miko said. "You're sitting around obsessing that Benny isn't speaking to you—but he's probably doing the same thing. What's the big deal about just reaching out to the guy?"

I sighed. "Because I guess I've convinced myself he's going to break up with me," I told her. "Or that he already has. And I just keep thinking, isn't it better to not know than to find out definitively that I've been dumped and have to face it? Because I've thought and thought about this, and I really think that's what it comes down to. Much as it pains me to quote Shelby, I've heard her say that guys don't call you to break up with you—they just ignore you."

"Ugh, Shelby," Miko said.

"Why, what's going on?" I asked.

"Don't change the subject," Miko said sternly. "You and Benny have been a totally adorable couple—you haven't even had any fights, have you? I just don't understand why you would automatically leap to the conclusion that he's dumped you. Sorry, Paulie, but that's just kind of . . . dumb. And you are no dummy."

I sighed. "I guess," I said. "I think I still kind of have a lot of insecurity about Benny. Anyway, the damage is done. Even if he wasn't mad at me, he will be now. It's been, like, a week or something."

"Wrong again," Miko said, leaning forward and grabbing my book bag. She opened a little pocket on the side and pulled out my cell phone.

"Don't!" I cried.

"I'm not doing anything," she said, handing the

phone to me. "You are. Send the guy a text message right now."

I took the phone and stared at it like I didn't know what it was used for. "But . . . what do I say?"

"Say, 'Hey—is everything okay?' It's short and to the point. If you want to be more personal, say you're worried about him."

I swallowed, then opened the phone, opened Benny's contact, and typed a quick sentence.

> **Hey—just wondering if you are okay? Kind of worried about you.**

I turned the phone to face Miko, who leaned forward and read it.

"Perfect. Now hit send," she told me.

I stared at her.

"The nice little green button. Push it one time with your finger," Miko coaxed, like she was talking to a puppy.

I did it. A cloud of butterflies erupted in my stomach.

"Okay. It's done."

"Yay," Miko said. "Don't you feel better already?"

"No!" I exclaimed. "I'm even more nervous now! I've gone from thinking I'm not going to hear from him to being terrified I'm going to hear from him any second! Ugh, let's just change the subject. So what did you mean about Shelby before?"

"Oh," Miko said, making a face. "She's just really getting on my nerves. She tries to be so supercompetitive about things, and at the same time, it's like she hardly knows me at all anymore. She didn't even come to my recital. I couldn't believe that! She knew how important that was to me. And she didn't apologize. She was just all defensive about having some other commitment and no ride. That really hurt my feelings. To be honest, I feel like we're not really even friends anymore. And now she's pulling something weird with the cover competition."

"Weird how?" I asked.

There was a knock on Miko's door, and Miko's mother popped her head inside.

"Oh, hello, Paulina," she said. "I didn't realize Miko still had company. Miko, your father just got home, and he'd like to speak to you."

Miko stood up quickly, and so did I.

"I'm sorry—I lost track of the time," I said. "Is it already six? I'm going to be late to meet Ivy."

"You still have a few minutes," Miko said. "Don't worry."

"Nice to see you, Mrs. Suzuki," I said.

She gave me a little pat on the arm as I walked out of Miko's bedroom. "You're welcome anytime, Paulina," she said warmly.

I followed Miko down the back staircase and into the kitchen. Her father was sitting at the table reading a newspaper. He looked surprised when he saw me, but he said hello.

"Hi, Mr. Suzuki," I said. "I just stopped by to give Miko a book she needs for school."

"So, thanks for the loan," Miko said.

"You're welcome," I told her. "Oops, I didn't actually give it to you! Hang on."

I unzipped my book bag, feeling awkward. The copy of *Animal Farm* was right on top, and I handed it to her.

"I'm just going to walk Paulie to the door, Dad," Miko said. "Be right back."

She followed me into the front hall and held my book bag while I pulled on my coat and hat. Before I put on my gloves, I checked my phone.

"He hasn't answered yet," I said.

Miko rolled her eyes. "It's been less than five minutes! Paulie, promise me you will not obsess about this all night."

"Miko?" her father called from the kitchen.

"I'll try," I said, opening the front door.

Miko gave me a quick hug. "Thanks for everything," she said. "Say hi to Ivy for me."

I smiled, opening the door all the way and wincing at the blast of frigid air on my face.

I was about to close the door when I remembered something.

"Hey, Miko, I forgot to ask if you have it!"

"Have what?" she asked, shooting a quick look over her shoulder and rubbing her hands over her arms against the cold.

"Perfect pitch."

"Miko!" her father called again.

Miko put her hand on the door and began to close it, but before it was quite shut she smiled and said, "As a matter of fact, I do."

· chapter ·

8

"Hey, there you are!" Ivy called out to me as I came through the door of the pizza place, stunned by the transition from cold to warm. She had snagged a little booth by the window. "Are you okay?"

"Sorry," I said. "I had to stop over at Miko's. I would have texted on the way here, but I couldn't stand to take my gloves off for even a second."

"No, that's fine," Ivy said. "It's just that you're, like, never late—I'm used to you being the first to arrive. So you went to Miko's?"

"I did," I said with a grin, sliding into the booth and unzipping my coat. "She needed a book for English. And now I've finally seen the inside of her house and lived to tell the tale. Her room is so cute. You'd love it. Oh, do we need to order?"

Ivy shook her head, pushing a soda toward me. "Nope—I just figured we were getting the same thing we always get. Small mushroom pizza and 7UP."

"Argh, I'm becoming all predictable like my mother. She always takes me and Kevin to the same restaurant, and she always orders the exact same thing. I always want to yell, 'Mom! Live a little!'"

Ivy laughed.

"Well, a mushroom pizza and 7UP is a perfect meal. Why mess with perfect?" she asked. "If you're becoming predictable, that means I am, too. So listen, did Miko seem okay?"

"She looks tired," I said. "And I know she's stressed. She was explaining all the stuff she has to prepare for this audition—it really is a lot."

"And her dad is really riding her, huh?" Ivy asked.

"He is," I said. "Honestly, though, she's pushing herself pretty hard, too. I'll just be glad when this whole thing is behind her."

"How long does she have again?"

"A week and a half," I replied.

"That's gonna be a long week and a half," Ivy said. "And that's around the time we should be making sure all our text is in final. I figure the last official thing we need to do is judge the cover competition. Tally swears up and down she's already started her piece—the one on collaboration and Drama Club. Mine is done, thank you very much. Two hundred words on collaboration and the classroom. Why learning in a group environment is such an important part of our education—that figuring out how to work with our classmates and teachers will prepare us to work well in different job environments with different kinds of bosses, and how the world would be a different place if we were all homeschooled until college. That kind of thing."

"Leaving me with what I thought would be the easy one—collaboration with each other," I said. "Which I need to do without overlapping any of the stuff you covered. It's supposed to be how we create a support system for each other, not as friends, 'cause everybody has those—but student to student. You know, like how there's just a kind of understanding that people should have each other's backs at school because we're all in it together. Which may end up a partial work of fiction, since I can't think of ANY instances where there isn't at least one person stirring the pot instead of making things better. Not that I'm naming PQuits."

"Ha," Ivy said. "Well, that's good. We don't want to sugarcoat anything. Just don't leave it to the last minute—you end up making yourself nuts, and me too."

A bell rang up by the counter, and someone called out, "Scanlon—small mushroom-cheese!"

Ivy stood up, gave a little bow like she'd just won something, and went to the counter to retrieve our pizza.

"See?" she asked as she placed it on the table. "No reason to mess with perfect."

The pizza smelled delicious. In the same moment I was realizing how hungry I was, my phone chimed—text-message alert. I glanced at it, and all thoughts of food hastily fled.

"Oh boy," I said.

"What?" Ivy asked. "Paulina, you look like you just saw a ghost. Who's the text from? Oh my gosh, is it finally Benny?"

I nodded. "Miko convinced me to send him a text asking if everything was okay," I said, my stomach flipping and my head spinning. It was here, on my phone. Finally. One way or the other, I had to face what was going on in Benny Novak's mind. I stared at the phone in terror, like someone had just told me it was wired to explode.

Ivy turned both palms to the ceiling and gave me a quizzical look.

"Um, I've been telling you to do that for a week," she said. "Then Miko suggests it, and you do it? Thanks a lot."

"It was kind of a buildup," I said hastily. "You telling me to do it all those times, then Miko saying the same thing. It was a collaboration!" I added.

"Uh-huh, right. It was research for *4 Girls*," Ivy said, grinning. "Whatever. The suspense is killing me—are you going to read it?"

I pressed the button to open Benny's text, read it once, read it again, and shook my head. *Really?* I took a breath and read it out loud to Ivy.

> **I'm fine, but I was kind of worried about you too—never heard back from you over Christmas.**

"See?" Ivy said. "A misunderstanding!"

"Yeah, but what does he mean he never heard back from me?" I asked. "I thought I was waiting to hear back from him!"

Ivy pointed at the phone. "Ask," she commanded.

> **OMG, so confused, sorry! Thought I was waiting to hear from you???**

I sent the text, then showed it to Ivy.

"When are you ever going to start listening to me?" Ivy chided. "How many times did I tell you this was all a misunderstanding, my nervous, misguided Anxiety Blob of a best friend?"

"A billion," I said, staring very hard at my phone as if I could force Benny's response to appear faster if I just concentrated enough.

"Which was not enough, apparently," she said. "You needed a billion and ONE."

"You laid all the groundwork," I told Ivy. "Miko just pushed me over the edge. She took my phone and said she was making me text him."

Another chime from my phone.

> **There was a note with the present— didn't you see it?**

Ivy and I stared at each other.

"Okay, wait, what present?" she asked.

"I have no idea! He never gave me a Christmas present! This is so weird," I said, typing while I talked.

> **Even more confused. Don't have a note or a present . . .**

"None of this makes sense," I said to Ivy. "What do you think?"

Ivy took a bite of pizza and chewed thoughtfully. *How can you eat at a moment like this!* I wanted to shout.

"Is it possible," she asked after taking a moment to blot her lips with her napkin, "that he left something and your mom brought it in and forgot about it?"

"No, definitely not," I replied. "She would never do that. Plus, she knows I've been kind of in limbo and wondering what's going on with Benny."

"You told her?" Ivy asked.

"I mentioned it," I said. "I mean, she obviously noticed that I suddenly had no plans with him or anything."

"And what did she say?"

I sighed. "That I should just ask him what was going on," I admitted.

"So you were told a billion and *two* times," Ivy said. "Hah."

"Okay, okay," I mumbled. "So I was an idiot. But you have to admit this is all kind of confusing."

"What if he left something and Kevin brought it in and lost it?" Ivy suggested.

I shook my head. "No way," I said. "Once over the summer Kevin brought the mail in and carried it up to his room and totally forgot about it, and there was some important bill there or something and when my mother finally uncovered it in his room, she was really mad. He was, like, basically banned for life from ever opening the mailbox again."

The phone chimed.

Too weird—I left you a package and note in your mailbox, like, over a week ago! At movies right now with parents, and it's about to start—will text you when it's over.

I started laughing. I still didn't know what had happened, but whatever it was—Benny was not breaking up with me! There was no other girl he liked better! He wasn't even mad at me! I was so giddy with relief I could hardly text—I kept hitting the wrong keys.

> **That is weird, but we will solve this mystery! Have fun at the movies!!**

"I am so happy." I beamed. "Benny got me a present!"

"Yeah, but where is it?" Ivy asked. "Call your mom."

I glanced at the time—she was coming to pick me up at seven, anyway. But it was only six thirty. I hit her contact on the speed dial, and she answered on the first ring.

"Hi, sweetie—are you done already?" she asked.

"Not really, but Mom, I finally heard from Benny, and he said he left me a package and a note in the mailbox over a week ago. But there was no package, right?"

"No, of course not," my mother told me. "I wouldn't have forgotten to tell you something like that. So you guys are finally talking—that's wonderful!"

"I know, but I'm just so confused," I said. "And he was about to go into a movie, so he couldn't really talk. But he did definitely say he left something. I guess it's possible he had the wrong house?"

That seemed unlikely, though. Benny had been to my house more than once—it looked nothing like our neighbor's.

"Or maybe he didn't have the wrong house," my mother said suddenly. "Just the wrong mailbox. I have an idea—I'm going to run and check—I'll call you right back."

"Okay!" I said, suddenly understanding what she meant. I hit the "end call" button.

"What?" Ivy asked.

"Well, you know that brick wall that separates our driveway from the Hendersons'? It was built with this little door in it on the end facing the street—it looks like a teeny oven or something. They probably meant for it to be a mailbox, but the mailbox we use is the copper one hanging outside the front door. But once we had a different mailman for a few days, and he kept leaving the mail down there. My mom thinks maybe Benny thought that was our mailbox, too. She just went to check! Oh my gosh, I hope she calls back soon—I am dying!"

Ivy took another huge bite of pizza. "Honestly, I don't know when your life got so complicated," she told me. "This is the kind of thing that usually happens to Tally, not you!"

"You're all beginning to rub off on me," I said. "Maybe I'll start taking violin lessons, too."

"Yeah, and you could audition for the next Drama Club production," Ivy suggested, giving me a wicked smile.

"Sometimes I feel like I'm already IN a Drama Club production," I told my friend. "Come on, phone, RING!"

"Take a deep breath and have some pizza," Ivy said. "The only thing worse than worrying is worrying on an empty stomach."

My phone rang, saving me from explaining that I couldn't eat a bite at the moment if my life depended on it.

"Mom?" I said a little breathlessly.

"What's she saying? Put her on speaker," Ivy said, talking over the sound of my mother's voice. I held up one finger.

"Paulie, just put her on speaker," Ivy said. "Now you're making me nuts."

"Really? Really? Okay, thanks!" I said. "Bye!"

Then I beamed at my best friend. "That's where it was," I said. "My mom just found it. Mailbox that isn't a mailbox. There's a package inside, with a card addressed to me."

Ivy's smile matched my own. She stood up. "I'm going to get this pizza wrapped up to go," she said.

An hour later, I was sitting in my room on my bed, the contents of Benny's package in my hand. The present itself, beautifully wrapped in red-and-gold paper, was a black velvet box containing a delicate necklace with a tiny heart-shaped charm. Inside the card Benny had created a handmade coupon that said:

> **THIS COUPON GOOD FOR ONE (1) HOLIDAY DINNER AT THE RESTAURANT OF YOUR CHOICE—CALL ME TO REDEEM THIS VALUABLE OFFER!**

No wonder he thought it was strange when I never called, I thought, holding the little necklace up so I could better admire it. A heart-shaped necklace and an offer for a fancy dinner, and for all he knew, I had just ignored them.

I had come such a long way since last year, when I suffered mostly in silence with the knowledge of my crush, rather than risk humiliation by actually trying to get to know Benny.

And after all that, I still picked saying nothing over taking a risk, I scolded myself. I'd come a long way in the confidence department, but I still had a lot of work to do in that department! My friends had been so right—all I had accomplished by putting my head in the sand was to create more confusion between me and Benny, not to mention an agonizing week at school. I couldn't wait to finally talk to him.

He called me as soon as the movie was out. I tried not to sound as giddy as I felt.

"And you're totally not the first person to make that mistake," I reassured Benny. "When the mailman goes on vacation, the guy filling in puts the mail in there sometimes."

"Still, I am so sorry," he told me earnestly. "I feel like an idiot—I don't know why I just didn't come out and say something when I didn't hear from you. Instead, I made you wait because I was too nervous to just ask. To be honest, I figured you hated the present, or . . . no offense, but maybe you had started liking somebody else, and the necklace just made everything worse . . ."

At that moment I truly believed Benny Novak was the sweetest guy that had ever lived.

"No, I should have said something to you," I said. "I'm the one that should feel like an idiot."

"Okay, I'll make you a deal," Benny said. "How about we both agree to forget we feel like idiots!"

"Awesome," I agreed, beaming. "And honestly, Benny, I love my present. The necklace is beautiful, and I would love to go to a restaurant with you. Though I guess it wouldn't exactly count as a holiday dinner anymore."

"Well, we'll make our own holiday—a new one," he said. "We'll call it Benny and Paulina Are Not Idiots Day."

"Yes, perfect," I said, laughing. "We'll have a blast celebrating that."

And hopefully, I added silently, *we will be celebrating it next year, too. And maybe even the year after!*

· chapter ·

9

Ivy winked at me as I walked into the art room on Monday morning. She had claimed our sunny table by the window again.

"So?" she asked as I carried my book bag over and tossed it heavily onto a chair. "Feet touching the ground yet?"

"Not quite," I said. "I'm still really happy."

"Oh, you have it on! Let me see it again!" Ivy exclaimed eagerly, spotting the little necklace I had on. I shot a look toward the door—only a few students had arrived so far, and Benny was not among them. I didn't want him to walk in and see me showing off the necklace. Or did I? Would a guy like that or not like it? I still had so much to figure out about this boyfriend thing!

"It's really pretty," Ivy said, reaching for the little heart pendant and holding it up. "And it looks great on you—that chain is just the right length. Good for Benny—he's got nice taste."

"Do you really like it?" I asked.

Oh no, I've turned into one of those gushing girls, I thought. But I really did want to know what Ivy thought of the necklace. Even though she had already told me fifteen times when she saw it Friday night.

"Yes," she said. "It's simple, elegant, and beautifully made. It's perfect for you."

There was a burst of laughter as several guys came into the classroom. I glanced nervously in their direction, and Ivy sat down and took out her art notebook, suddenly all business. *Awesome, Ivy*, I thought. She could totally read my mind. She knew I wanted to talk about Benny, but not until we were safely away from the classroom.

"Over fifteen cover submissions for the blog," Ivy said. "Considering there's almost another full week until the deadline, I think that's pretty good."

"I didn't even think we'd get that many," I said. "I bet the submitting anonymously thing really worked in our favor. People don't feel like they're taking a risk putting their work out there."

"I know, right?" Ivy asked. "Hey, did you talk to Miko over the weekend? I've sent her a couple of *4 Girls* things just to keep her in the loop, but no response."

I shook my head. "I sent her an e-mail, but she didn't answer it, either," I said. "I know she has violin lessons on Saturdays and extra coaching on Sundays. And she's got those extra lessons now on Tuesdays. She probably didn't have time."

There was a burst of laughter from a group of girls coming through the door. PQuits, of course, probably laughing because Shelby was laughing and they all fell in line behind her. They headed for their usual table, then Miko came in behind them. She didn't even glance at them. She came straight over to me and Ivy, one hand covering a giant yawn.

"Hey, Miko, how are you? You look tired," Ivy said.

"I am tired," Miko said. "Sorry I didn't get back to your e-mails, guys, especially the *4 Girls* stuff, but I just didn't have time. It always sounds so lame when people say that, but I seriously felt like I didn't have an off minute from Saturday morning until Sunday night."

If Miko noticed Shelby watching her with narrowed eyes, she gave no indication. I sure noticed it, though.

"Hey, no worries—it's fine," Ivy said. "We knew this was going to be supercrunch time for you. We've got it covered."

"Well, I did make a couple of notes about things I saw on the blog I wanted to pass on to you," Miko said, unzipping her book bag and pulling out a notebook. "I wrote down a few questions and one— oh, do not even tell me."

"What?" I asked.

Miko sighed and shook her head.

"This is my music-theory notebook. What a space cadet. I was so bleary this morning I grabbed the wrong book. I'm sorry, you guys—I am flaking out big-time."

"It's fine," I reassured her. "Don't worry about it!"

"Seriously," Ivy echoed. "If we think you're going to be stressing even one second about *4 Girls* on top of everything else you have to deal with right now, we're just going to feel guilty."

"Well, thanks," Miko said. "It's just another week, then I'll be back to normal."

I could see that Shelby was still watching Miko. Now she tossed her book bag onto the PQuit table, stood up, and headed toward us. Miko's back was to her, so she didn't notice.

"So how's the cover thing coming?" Shelby asked, pulling up a chair and plopping down with us as if we all hung out every day.

There was a moment of surprised silence. Miko didn't say anything.

"It's going well," Ivy said. "We've gotten a lot of good submissions."

"How many?" Shelby asked.

Ivy and I exchanged a look. We hadn't talked about whether the number of submissions should be public information or not. But the fact that Shelby wanted to know made me automatically NOT want to tell her. Ivy gave me a small nod of agreement, reading my thoughts as usual.

"A good number," Ivy said. "We're not being specific about it. We don't want people to feel like they shouldn't submit something now just because they think we have too many already."

Shelby looked at Miko, who was flipping through her music-comp book like she was looking for something very important.

"Seems like you should give more weight to the people who submitted right away," Shelby said. That caused Miko to look up.

"Why?" she asked. "That doesn't make any sense."

"Because it's more of a commitment to do it right away, before you even know if anyone else is participating," Shelby said.

Miko made an irritated sound and went back to flipping through her notebook.

"It's great that you submitted right away, Shelby," I began, "but we really won't know the specific order they came in—that's part of the whole idea of keeping the process anonymous. They just get assigned random identification code numbers. We'll be judging them all at once, and the less we know about who sent what when, the better."

"Mine's the one with the balloon," Shelby said.

"Shelby, what part of *anonymous* do you not understand?" Miko exclaimed. "Why do you have to act like the rules don't apply to you?"

"What rules?" Shelby asked. "Just because you run a contest doesn't make you the boss all of a sudden. Anyway, it would be totally obvious which one is mine."

"Not to me," Ivy said.

"Miko would know," Shelby said, giving Miko a hard look. Miko raised her eyes from her notebook and returned Shelby's gaze silently.

I thought about what Miko had told me on Friday. Not only was her friendship with Shelby unraveling, it appeared to be doing so right in front of my eyes. She had started to tell me something about Shelby and the submission, but she'd never finished. What on earth was going on?

Over Shelby's shoulder, I saw Tally come through the door talking a mile a minute to Benny. I felt a slight flush creep over my face. Benny's eyes immediately went to me, and he smiled. I smiled back. He dropped his book bag at his usual seat, but he walked over to us with Tally.

"Hey, guys," Benny said, looking utterly adorable in his lacrosse team jacket and his rumpled playing-in-a-windstorm hair.

"Hey, Benny," Ivy said.

"Hiya," I echoed, trying to make my smile slightly less galactic in size. We'd talked on the phone several times since the whole mystery was cleared up, but this was the first time I'd actually seen him since the whole Mystery of the Mailbox That Was Not a Mailbox had been solved.

"Hiya," Benny said back to me. The bell announcing the start of class rang, though Ms. Delacroix had not yet come into the room. "See you after class, Paulie," Benny said, giving me another smile that shot lightning bolts into my stomach before heading back to his table.

"No more trouble in paradise?" Shelby asked me. The look on her face made it clear that fact disappointed her. She *liked* trouble in paradise. Shelby Simpson really could be awful. I hated for Miko to have anything else to deal with, but the fact of the matter was I was thrilled she was finally reevaluating her former best friend.

"I thought I was going to be late!" Tally announced, dropping dramatically into her chair and doing a slight double take as she registered Shelby's presence at our table.

"You are late," Ivy told her.

"But Ms. Delacroix isn't here yet," Tally protested.

"Well, she's late, too," Ivy said.

"Only one of us can be late," Tally stated. "How come you're sitting with us, Shelby?"

I almost laughed at Tally's bluntness. She often spoke so fast she didn't have time to think about what came out of her mouth. This time, I was glad.

"I'm not," Shelby said, getting up abruptly just as our teacher came through the doorway.

"*Bonjour*, my students. I am sorry to be a little late," I heard Ms. Delacroix say in her singsong voice as she swept into the room. Shelby walked quickly back to her table. Miko stared at her notebook, her expression unreadable.

"Okay, so now we are going to get right to it. We will be working in watercolors. Today we are all painters. Before we start, I want to show you just a few pictures, so you can see that all watercolors do not look alike, depending on how you work with the paints. I will give you a few, what is it you like to call them—pointers—but mostly you will learn by doing and asking questions. It is more fun that way, *n'est-ce pas?*"

Ms. Delacroix opened her laptop. "Just a couple of things I have here on the PowerPoint. Can somebody please put out the light?"

Benny, who was sitting close to the door, got up and switched the lights off. The screen was filled with a white sailboat in a bright-blue ocean. Everything seemed lit from within, particularly the waves, which were almost transparent.

"That is Winslow Homer, very cheerful, yes? You see how much he lets the white of the paper create light and space? But all watercolors do not have to be in this style. See this painting by Edward Burne-Jones."

"Wow!" I said.

In the center of the painting was an angel with enormous wings hovering slightly over the ground, as three men stood on the left, each wearing beautiful flowing garments that were painted in such detail I could almost feel the fabric.

"Wow indeed, yes, Paulina? This is also watercolor, but see how rich the colors? Such a lush painter, such breathtaking detail. Very different from this style. This is Kandinsky."

I stared at the image on the screen, trying to figure it out. It was a collection of brightly colored shapes and renderings of a jumble of things. Every time I thought I recognized something—a rabbit, a pillow, a person—I would look again and see something different. Nothing in the painting made sense, but there was something about it that I liked.

"Okay, let's have the lights back on. I am happy to look at paintings all day long, but that is me. You will have more fun painting. Each table has a watercolor box—please open them. You will see you have a number of tubes of paint. If there is one you want to use, you can open it and squeeze a bit onto the tray, just like a little blob of toothpaste—that is a good size."

Miko opened the box on our table. For the first time the worried crease between her eyebrows disappeared. "These are such nice paints!" she said. "Look at this indigo. This is a killer color."

She unscrewed the cap from the small tube and squeezed a little of the paint onto the plastic paint tray. Ms. Delacroix was walking around placing large glasses of water on every table.

"You're not going to be able to paint very much with that teeny bit of paint," Tally said, squeezing a little red squiggle out onto another section of the paint tray.

"You mix it with a little water," Miko said. "It's a lot more paint than you think. The water gives it body. That why they're called watercolors."

There was a large pad of watercolor paper on my side of the table. I pulled out four pieces and handed them around.

"Is it just me, or does this paint smell really good?" Ivy asked.

"I *love* the smell of watercolors," Miko agreed. "See, look, Tal, if I dip the brush in the water, then dip it into the paint, look how much is really there."

Miko made a fanciful squiggle across the paper, in varying widths. Then she quickly rinsed the brush, dried it, dunked it into Tally's red paint, and added little curly designs that looked like confetti.

"See, if you don't use any water the paint is thicker and the color is more intense."

I opened a tube of orange paint, pausing to watch Miko finish up a red curlicue and wash her brush again.

"I love orange," she said, picking up some of that color with her brush and making little sunbursts between the curlicues.

"How are you doing that? How did you just do that?" Tally asked.

"Seriously," I agreed. "How do you come up with those designs?"

"I'm just playing around," Miko said.

"Now that you are finding your paints, let me give you a few little ideas," Ms. Delacroix said. "I can see some of you already mixing in a little water. This is good experimenting time to see how opaque or translucent you can make the color, yes? But also you can apply water to the paper first, then put the paint on. Watch what happens with that. We can create two different areas of color that will bleed into each other if they touch. Even if one color is dry, if the wet brush touches it, the color will melt and leak a little. This can be an interesting effect, or maybe just a mistake, *oui*? Also, please see that there are sponges in the paint box. These are for painting, not cleaning! Dip your sponge into some water, then the paint, and brush it across the paper or dab it on. You can create many different textures with watercolors. Or run the sponge over the whole page with one color for a background. We call that a wash."

I found one of the little sponges and dipped it in the orange paint, then tried to dab it onto the paper the way Ms. Delacroix had described. I ended up with a little row of orange blobs. Not very impressive, especially considering that Miko had now transformed her sunbursts and curlicues into something that looked like a surrealist surprise party.

"Remember when you apply the paint to the paper, it is going to dry looking lighter than it does when it is wet," Ms. Delacroix explained. "All of this you will see for yourselves as you experiment. Don't worry about if you are making a pretty picture or wasting paper. Today is for learning how the paint feels and what it does. Play with mixing colors, too— look what just a spot of blue added to red will do."

I couldn't help peeking to see what my friends were

doing. Ivy had drawn an intricate circular pattern that looked almost like a labyrinth, and she was carefully painting one section of it deep blue. Tally had created a large sunlike ball in the center of her paper, and was sponging water around it and adding little drops of red paint, creating the bleeding effect Ms. Delacroix had explained.

"Why does everyone else's look good?" I asked, frustrated. "Mine just looks like a squashed mango."

I hadn't really meant to share that with the whole class. I was more talking to myself, but Ms. Delacroix heard me and came over.

"This is the beauty of watercolors—they can always be transformed," she told me. "What if you soak a sponge in water and rub it over the paper?"

I tried it and was surprised to see I was able to smear my orange blobs into streaks of lighter orange. The paper was still very wet, and I tried dabbing a little solid blue on it. I was fascinated by the little river of color that appeared in streams of indigo.

"Ah!" Ms. Delacroix said. "Now it looks very different."

"It looks like a river," I said. "It's definitely better than the mango."

Ms. Delacroix walked behind Miko and watched her for a moment. Then someone at Benny's table knocked over their water and yelped, and our teacher dashed over to help clean it up before everyone's experiments were ruined.

I was amazed at how quickly the time passed. Though I expanded my river to little channels of purples and greens, I felt like I had just gotten started when the bell rang.

Miko gathered our brushes and cleaned them off, and Ivy closed the tubes of paint and tossed them back in the box.

"I'll put the rest of this stuff away," Miko said. "I want to ask Ms. Delacroix about something, anyway."

"Okay, if you want," Ivy said. Miko looked up and nodded. She shot a quick glance in Shelby's direction. Shelby was leaning in close to Daphne and whispering something. They were both staring at Miko. Both of them began to laugh very loudly. Miko flinched slightly and returned her attention to the brushes.

I suddenly felt guilty. Here I was feeling happy that Miko was on the outs with Shelby, but the situation was obviously upsetting to Miko. Shelby was not being nice. And knowing Shelby, the more the friendship fell apart, the meaner she would be. They had been friends for a long time. It had to hurt. *I've got to be more sympathetic*, I told myself.

For now, the best thing seemed to be to leave Miko to her tidying.

"Okay, Ivy and Tal—we ready?" I asked cheerfully.

"My mother says a person should always be ready for anything, and I just don't see how that's possible," Tally said, tucking a strand of hair behind her ear. "I could carry a good book and a flashlight and a bathing suit everywhere, but then what if *anything* meant space travel? Or something requiring sunblock? Or meeting the president?"

Ivy took Tally by the arm and led her toward the door.

"Are these the kind of thoughts that keep you up at night?" Ivy asked, looking over her shoulder at me and giving me a wink.

"Oh no," Tally said. "What keeps me up at night is worrying one day I might accidentally end up in a play on opening night and not know any of my lines, or not even know what play I'm in, and be in my pajamas, and not know there is an audience until they start laughing at me!"

"How do you *accidentally* end up in a play?" I asked, shaking my head in wonder at the ever-stunning imagination of Tally Janeway.

"Oh, it happened to someone I know!" Tally said, taking a deep breath to prepare to tell the story.

That's when I noticed that Benny was waiting in the hall. I felt the sun come out right there in the corridor, and everything looked twice as bright.

"Oh, hey," he said to me. "Walk you to your next class?"

I nodded happily.

"Great!" I replied.

Tally's story would have to wait.

· chapter ·
10

"Will you please look at Tally?" Ivy said, pointing out the window.

Ivy and I had snagged a window booth at Kauffee Haus, which was always packed, even on a Wednesday after school.

I looked in the direction Ivy was pointing. Tally was trudging down the freshly shoveled sidewalk, wrapped in multiple layers. She had a pair of panda bear–shaped earmuffs on over her hat, and her scarf was wrapped so many times around her head, she looked like a fashionably scattered mummy whose wrappings were beginning to unfurl. As we watched her, giggling, the heel of her snow boot slid forward on a patch of ice as she tried to put something in her purse. She spun around, almost dropping the purse, then regained her balance. Unable to get the purse opened, she removed a mitten, then a glove underneath the mitten—both of which dropped into a snowbank separating the sidewalk from the street.

"I wish Miko could see this," I said. "It seems like she can barely even leave her house anymore."

"But it's just until the audition, right?" Ivy asked. "Five more days?"

"I guess so," I said. Tally was still fumbling around outside.

"What is she doing?" I asked, shaking my head. "Putting her phone away? Why not wait till she gets inside? Does she realize she's standing right outside the door?"

Ivy tapped on the glass. "Tally!" she called. "Tally!"

Tally continued her fumbling, totally oblivious to us. She had managed to pick up her glove, but her mitten was blowing down the sidewalk, and she was running after it.

"Gloves AND mittens—she really takes the cake. Is she ever going to actually make it inside?" I asked.

"Well, she's already fifteen minutes late," Ivy said good-naturedly. "It's a good excuse for me to have another cappuccino."

"I'll stick with hot chocolate," I said, waving at the waitress.

"Let's get a couple of those chocolate croissants, too," Ivy suggested. "It's, like, twenty degrees outside. Our bodies need the extra fuel."

I didn't know if there was any scientific basis for that claim, but I didn't care. Chocolate croissants sounded awesome. The waitress, a slim dark-haired girl who looked about college age, hurried over and gave me a look that said, "I'm crazy busy—hurry up."

"Two hot chocolates, a cappuccino, and three chocolate croissants," I said. "Please."

"You got it," the waitress said, speeding off.

"Three, huh?" Ivy asked, looking amused. "You seem pretty confident Tally's actually going to make it through the door."

Right on cue, the door burst open and Tally rushed through, as if she was being pursued by a pack of wolves. She looked around the café wildly, not noticing for several moments that Ivy and I were both waving and saying, "Tally, over here."

"Oh, there you are!" Tally exclaimed, looking startled to see us sitting right there, as if we'd just beamed down from the Starship *Enterprise* and materialized in front of her. "I am so sorry I'm late. I forgot my wallet, and Mom had to drive all the way back home, and then she dropped me on the corner so she wouldn't have to drive around the block because of the one-way street, and when I got out of the car, my boot got stuck in the snowdrift, and when I tried to pull my leg up, the boot came off, and I had to stand balanced with one foot in the air like the guy in *Karate Kid* while I tried to pull the boot out before I lost my balance and put my bare foot in the snow, because when the boot came off, the sock came off, too! And the whole time I had my phone in my hand because if I don't hold it sometimes I forget where it is, and by the time I got my boot back on, my hands were so cold I kept dropping the rest of my stuff, and then a big wind came!"

"Tally," Ivy said. "Breathe. You're safe now. And look—we have chocolate!"

Tally turned to see where Ivy was pointing. Our waitress was on her way over with three steaming mugs and three delicious-looking pastries.

"Oh, thank goodness." Tally exhaled, sinking into the spot next to Ivy, piling her things on the seat between them. She wrapped her hands around the mug of hot chocolate and sighed. "It's *sooo* good to feel warm again," she said.

"Well, not to . . . um, snow on your parade, but I'm going to have to go before too long," Ivy said. "So we should probably get the *4 Girls* stuff taken care of. Let's talk Collaboration Concepts articles. We've got more than enough submissions, and I think we're good with those two poems, the cafeteria review—which the person didn't exactly link to the collaboration theme, but I've solved that by creating a little area on the blog where everyone can either give their own thoughts on the review or write about what they'd personally like to see changed in the menu. Then there are the two short stories, and the essay on team sports and how the right kind of support from your teammates can actually make you a better athlete. Haven't seen either of your articles, though. I, as usual, finished mine ahead of schedule—but you know that because I so efficiently e-mailed it to you Monday night. Oh, PLEASE hold your applause, ladies and gentlemen. You are too kind."

"Ha," I said. "Okay, I'm sorry about not getting mine in by last night. The thing is, I was having a tough time with 'collaborating with each other.' I was trying to write about art class because we're all in that one, and it's kind of a class and interacting with each other at the same time, but I just wasn't getting a good line on it, you know what I mean? So here's the thing—if you still want me to stick with the original subject, I will—I'll figure it out and get it done. I mean, I have a version of it done—I'm just not happy with it. But I've been thinking a lot about something Miko said when I was at her house last Friday, about feeling this pressure to decide what path she wants to take right now. And I wrote something about it."

"It doesn't matter to me if you don't stick to the original topic," Ivy said. "But I didn't get your article—did you e-mail it?"

"No," I said, unzipping my purse. "But I printed it out after school, and I brought it with me. Want to hear it?"

"We were supposed to bring our articles?" Tally asked, her hand freezing with the croissant halfway to her mouth.

"Nope," Ivy said. "We were supposed to have e-mailed them to each other by last night. But don't worry," she added as Tally opened her mouth to say something. "We still have time. Can you get it to us by tonight?"

"I swear it—I pinkie swear it—I solemnly vow to," Tally promised, looking hugely relieved and finally taking the bite of pastry.

"Okay, here goes," I said, unfolding a piece of paper and setting it on the table in front of me.

Collaborating with Our Selves

I have a friend who happens to be really good at a number of things. I won't get into specifics, but let's just say when the Universe was handing out gifts, she got a nice little pile of them. Because of that, there are a lot of things she could potentially end up doing with her life. For most of us, worrying about what we're going to do for a living will come later, maybe when we're much older, or in college. Maybe not until after that. But for someone who has an exceptional talent or talents, the pressure might come earlier and faster. The other day, my friend said, "I'm thirteen years old—am I really supposed to know without a doubt who I want to be yet?" And that got me thinking. To me, the very obvious answer to that question is no.

The theme of this issue of *4 Girls* is Collaboration Concepts. The dictionary tells us that the word *collaboration* means to work jointly with others or together. By now, we have learned to collaborate in many different ways—at home with our parents and siblings, at school with our classmates and teachers, and out in public, at restaurants or stores or camp. Most of us have come to know what people expect of us and what the best way is to meet their expectations.

But what about what we expect of ourselves or more precisely our "selves"? Collaboration, even cooperation, is kind of an awkward word to use when we're talking about our selves. It's probably more accurate to say we need to be true to our selves. And what does that mean? To me, it means making sure our own voices, our own wishes, and our own dreams don't get lost in the expectations of other people. There is no single perfect path for any one person. But at any given time, there will be one that seems the most like home. The place or job in life that, when I imagine doing it, feels like "me." And what feels the most right to us might change a lot from one year to the next. So when I think about my friend and her question, I want to say again, "No—you are NOT supposed to know without a doubt who you are right now."

My mom asked me what I was writing about for this month's *4 Girls*. When I told her, she gave me one of her favorite quotes by a famous psychiatrist and philosopher named Carl Jung. I liked it so much, I wanted to end with it here, and with a reminder to all of us to remember that our dreams and our expectations are just as important as anyone else's. Because as Dr. Jung said, "The privilege of a lifetime is to become who you truly are."

I folded up the paper and looked at my friends. Ivy was shaking her head.

"You don't like it?" I asked, disappointed.

"I'm shaking my head because I can't think of anything wrong with it," Ivy said. "I love it. Except for the title—'Collaborating with Our Selves' is pretty blah. Maybe try to come up with something catchier?"

"I think it's a great article, too!" Tally said. "It's kind of like what I wrote about in the first issue, about how I would hate to have to play the same part in the same play for the rest of my life."

"Exactly, Tally," I said. "I thought of that when I was writing it. Okay, I'm so glad. The reason I didn't e-mail it to everyone is I wanted to see if you guys thought it was any good first. And if you did, then I would send it to Miko to see if she was okay with us using it. Since, obviously, the 'friend' I'm talking about is her."

"Definitely send it to her," Ivy said. "I'm sure she'll like it as much as we do."

"It's so much better than mine," Tally said wistfully.

"I thought you hadn't finished yours yet," Ivy said.

"I haven't—but it's so much better than mine is going to be when it's finished," Tally corrected herself.

Ivy smiled and checked her watch.

"Uh-oh, my mom is going to be by to pick me up really soon—she's taking me shopping. So the one

135

other piece of *4 Girls* business we need to talk about is the e-mail from Ms. Delacroix that came today. You guys both got it, right?"

I nodded, pulling up the e-mail on my phone to glance at it one more time.

▼ **From:** DelacroixS

▼ **To:** Fashion Maven, IvyNYC, StarQuality, Paulina M. Barbosa

▼ **Subject:** 4 Girls cover judging

Hello, girls, here is your friendly faculty adviser checking in with you. I have made a note in my calendar that the deadline for the cover competition is on Sunday, four days from today. I am wondering if you would like to come to my house that day— we could have a little get-together and some refreshments, and take the time to look at each picture. If you have no time for this in your schedule, we can of course each review the pictures by ourselves. You can let me know anytime.—Madame Delacroix

"Oh, that was so nice of her," Tally exclaimed. "Y'all, I've never been to a teacher's house before. When I was little, I thought teachers lived at school."

"I saw it, too—to be honest, I'm assuming Miko is going to be a no on this because the first part of her audition is the next day," I said.

"That's what I figured, too," Ivy said. "And if we can't all go, then we probably shouldn't do it."

I nodded, relieved to have an excuse to say no other than the fact that Ms. Delacroix still made me feel nervous, like I was being silently judged and found wanting.

"So we just need to run that by Miko, then one of us can send her an e-mail saying no thanks," Ivy said. "Do you want to send Miko a text?"

"I'll just leave her a voice mail," I said, hitting Miko's contact number on my phone. I was surprised when Miko answered.

"Hey, it's Paulie!" I said. "I know you're about to have your extra lesson—just quickly wanted to ask if you'd seen the e-mail Ms. Delacroix sent about Sunday?"

"Yes, I did—I figured that's what you were calling about," Miko answered.

"Okay, good—well, we assumed you wouldn't be able to go because of your audition the next day, which is totally fine. One of us can just—"

"No, I want to go," Miko said. "I am going!"

I hesitated, surprised. "Oh," I said. "I mean . . . are you sure?"

"What is she saying?" Ivy mouthed. I held up one finger.

"I am totally sure," Miko said. "Remember at my house when you told me that sometimes I have to remember what I want, too—that every once in a while I should take a stand? You meant that, right?"

I glanced at my article, still folded on the table.

"Of course," I said. What was Miko going to do?

"Well, this is what I'm taking a stand over. I really want to go to Ms. Delacroix's house. She's really cool, and I like her a lot, and this is an amazing chance for me to get to know her better, and maybe to see her studio and her work. I can be done in time for my final coaching session that afternoon. So I told my dad, 'Look—I've been working like a crazy person getting ready for this audition, and there's nothing I can do on Sunday morning while practicing that's going to change how well I know the material.' I told him going to this teacher's house was really important to me. And he looked kind of surprised, but he said okay!"

"Wow!" I said. "Good for you, Miko. Um, hang on one minute." I turned to Ivy and Tally. "So, Miko actually CAN go on Sunday. And she really, really WANTS to go—she basically stood up to her father about it."

"Really? Go, Miko," Ivy said. "Okay then, sure!

I like the idea of us all being together to go over the submissions—more collaboration and all that."

"I want to go, just to be able to say I've seen the inside of a teacher's house," Tally said. "I wonder if they—"

I smiled at Tally as I went back to the phone.

"Hey, Miko, okay, we'll do it. Ms. Delacroix said anytime, so what works with your schedule?"

"My last coaching session is at three," Miko said. "And I can just bring my violin with me, so how about noon? That would still leave me time to get in a few hours of practicing that morning, and then I can let my fingers rest during the meeting."

"Okay," I told her. "I'll set it up."

"Oh, yay, I'm really psyched about this!" Miko said. "But wow, look at the time. I gotta run! Talk later!"

I hung up and tossed the phone on the table. "Okay, looks like we're going to Ms. Delacroix's house after all," I said.

And I tried to look happy about it.

· chapter ·

11

I sat in the middle of the backseat of the Scanlons' Land Rover, between Miko and Tally, who as usual was talking a mile a minute.

"I mean, think about it—what if we suddenly all had to live outside?" Tally asked. "Like, what if there were no more houses or anything, and we could only have nests or dens like animals do, and it was still this cold out. Don't you ever wonder how the rabbits and the deer do it? How do they stay warm? How do they sleep in the snow?"

"Well, you have a point," Mrs. Scanlon said as she drove. "Humans have been slowly adapting for thousands of years. At some point, early humans developed the ability to use natural resources like caves as shelter, and eventually they became intelligent enough to build their own shelters wherever they wanted. The elements were kept at bay a bit. Over generations we lost layers of fat and hair that would have kept us warmer."

"Thank goodness we lost them," Ivy said. "I don't want extra layers of fat and hair, thank you very much."

Mrs. Scanlon laughed. "It does make us a little more vulnerable to the elements, though," she said. "Fortunately, our brains evolved, too, and we've gotten very good at building warm houses and heating systems. Oh, I think this should be her driveway. She's really out in the woods here. What a beautiful spot."

We had been driving on a country road in a heavily wooded area for almost ten minutes without seeing another house. Now we were turning into a drive flanked on either side by an old stone wall. I saw a mailbox that said DELACROIX on the side. The road ended in a small dirt turnaround just beyond the driveway.

"Yes, this is definitely it," I said. "She said the street was a dead end, so we couldn't accidentally drive past her house."

"Must be tough in all this snow," Ivy's mother remarked as we drove up the steep driveway. "This driveway is all uphill."

The driveway wound around, making a leisurely path up the hill. Finally we came to a break in the trees, and the house came into view.

"It's beautiful!" remarked Mrs. Scanlon.

It was very pretty. The small house was set into the side of the hill and was made of stone and weathered brown clapboard. It looked very old. On one side there were more modern-looking additions with huge windows. In the center of the house was a large stone chimney, and smoke poured out of it.

"Wow," Miko said. "I would love to live in a house like this. It must be so quiet out here all the time."

We got out of the car, and the smell of smoke filled the air—a delicious, cozy scent. The sun was very bright, and the top layer of snow on the walkway had melted into a layer of slush. The front door opened, and Ms. Delacroix came out, waving at us as she walked toward the car.

"Hello, *mes élèves*! Welcome, my students!" she said. "And you are Ivy's mother? Thank you so much for driving them."

"Yes, I'm Karen Scanlon. I was happy to drive them over," Mrs. Scanlon said. "What a beautiful house—nineteenth century?"

"Yes, that's right," Ms. Delacroix said. "The oldest part was built in 1870."

"I'll be back to pick three of you up at two thirty," Mrs. Scanlon said. "Miko, are you absolutely sure you don't want me to drive you to your lesson? It seems silly for your dad to make the trip when I'm picking everyone else up."

"Thanks," Miko said. "But my dad insisted on driving me. He's going to come a bit earlier, at around two. He's worried I'll be late or something."

"Okay, then," Mrs. Scanlon said. "If he changes his mind, let me know. I'm always on time. Ivy can vouch for that. Have fun, guys!"

As Mrs. Scanlon got back into her car, Tally was shivering dramatically and jumping from foot to foot.

"It's even colder outside your house than it is outside mine!" she told Ms. Delacroix.

"Then let's go inside by the nice warm fire," Ms. Delacroix said. "Be careful not to slip—the sun has melted the snow a little, but the temperature is dropping and there is some ice."

We followed our teacher through the heavy wooden front door into a small hallway with old, wide-planked wooden floors that creaked under our feet. Ms. Delacroix led us into a large, simply furnished living room, where a fire was burning in a large stone fireplace. Tally immediately went over to it and held her hands out to warm them, while Miko, Ivy, and I took off our coats and hung them on some pegs by the door. The furniture in the living room was mostly wooden and antique looking, except for a large, fat sofa and chair near the fire. The walls were covered with prints and photographs and paintings. My eye was drawn immediately to a photograph near the fireplace.

"Please, get comfortable, warm yourselves like Tally, and be at home here," Ms. Delacroix said. "I have made us a pot of sweet tea—I'm just going to go and fetch it."

I walked over toward the fireplace to get a better look at the photograph. At first I thought it was a tree in the center of a field, under a sky filled with sun and clouds. But when I looked closer, I realized that the field was actually made of clouds, too, so that the tree seemed suspended at a point between two skies. Off to one side, a small human figure was walking through the clouds. I wasn't sure if the person was walking toward the tree or away from it. It made me think of the first time I had ever flown in an airplane and how captivated I was by the sight of the carpet of clouds that looked like miles of cotton candy going off in every direction.

"Do you need any help?" Ivy called toward the kitchen. Ms. Delacroix appeared in the doorway holding a tray of steaming mugs.

"Thank you, Ivy, but it is all ready. Let's all sit and have a nice, warm drink. We get relaxed and comfortable first, then we can talk shop, as you say it, and Miko can have that look at my studio she asked for."

The couch was big enough for all four of us. Ms.

Delacroix sat on the armchair after handing each of us a mug of steaming tea.

"Your house is so nice," Ivy said. "I live in an old house, too. I didn't think I would like it when we moved here from the city, but I do. I love old houses now."

"I love them, too, Ivy," she replied. "I have always lived in old houses, since I was a little girl. And never, ever do I have carpets. I must have the feel of the wood under my feet. It makes me feel as if I am really here, really home."

I wished that I could think of something to say. Everyone else looked comfortable and at ease. I didn't want to say something that would make me sound stupid. *Why do I care?* I wondered. *She's just a teacher.*

"Do you live here all alone?" Tally asked.

Ivy nudged Tally.

"Ow!" she protested. "What did I say wrong?"

"That's kind of a personal question," Ivy whispered.

"No, it isn't," Tally shot back. "I mean, is it? I guess it is. Are personal questions bad? But in a way, aren't all questions personal, I mean, if you're asking a person something?"

"It's okay," Ms. Delacroix said, smiling at Tally. "Yes, I live here by myself. My husband died eight years ago. After a while I felt I should be in a smaller

145

house, and I moved here. Last summer, I decided I would like to start teaching again. I so enjoy middle school."

She took a sip of tea, her gaze directed at the fire. I thought of how quiet the house would be when she was in it alone. What was it like to live by yourself, with no family? The thought suddenly made me feel sad.

"Did you always know you wanted to be an artist?" Miko asked. "Or were you ever torn between doing that and something else?"

"Well, Miko, I have been an artist from my very earliest memory. It's just the way I was born. All my life I have drawn, painted, sculpted. But if you mean how long I have been painting as a profession, to sell and exhibit and improve my craft, then only about twenty years. Before that, in Paris, I was a nurse."

"You were a nurse?" Tally asked.

"Oh yes," she replied. "And I loved that, too."

"They seem like such completely different jobs," I said. Well, I had finally managed to say something.

"Yes, you are quite right, Paulina," she agreed. "And yet many of the experiences I had and the people I met when I was a nurse influenced my painting."

"That's kind of like what Paulina wrote about in her article for the upcoming issue," Tally said. "Right, Paulina?"

"Right," I said, glancing at Miko. "It's not quite done yet, though. I might need to fix a few things."

I had forgotten to ask Miko what she thought of the article, which I'd e-mailed to her last night. She hadn't said anything about it on the ride over.

For someone who had been so excited about visiting Ms. Delacroix, Miko seemed kind of subdued. She didn't even seem to have heard what Tally said. She kept looking at something on the wall over my shoulder. When I turned to look, I saw a clock.

She's nervous about the time, I thought. *About her coaching session.*

"This tea was really good," I said. "I'm feeling ready to go over the submissions—how about you guys?"

"Oh, I just started feeling warm and comfortable," Tally complained. "Do we have to?"

"Well, there is no need to rush because of me," Ms. Delacroix said.

"Um, actually, Miko has a commitment later this afternoon," I said. "That's why I was thinking maybe we should do our *4 Girls* work sooner rather than later."

"Ah, yes, you said your father is coming to take you to a lesson," Ms. Delacroix said.

"It's my last . . . well, it's a coaching session, actually," Miko said. "An extra one. I play the violin."

"Ah, yes, I noticed you carrying something with you.

Very well, then, let's get started now. If you want to come with me into my studio, I have a computer there with a very large monitor," Ms. Delacroix said. She stood up.

Tally was right—it was very tempting to stay near the warm fire. But I got to my feet right away to follow our teacher. Miko stood up, too, and shot me a quick, grateful look.

"Thank you," she mouthed. I winked at her.

We walked through a wide doorway into a bright, modern-looking room.

I looked around curiously at Ms. Delacroix's studio. It seemed there were more windows than walls in the room, and the high wooden ceiling had two enormous skylights built in. There was a large worktable in the center of the room, on which paints and brushes were organized neatly. In one corner was a large rack where finished canvases were stacked. By one window close to the door was an easel with a canvas sitting on it, which I guessed was the painting Ms. Delacroix was working on now.

It seemed rude to just walk by the painting without saying anything, so I stopped.

"This is pretty," I said. I wasn't just trying to be nice—I really liked it. *Pretty* seemed like a stupid word to use, though. People were pretty. Outfits were pretty. Were paintings?

The painting was a winter scene of an old, weathered barn sitting on the edge of a snowfield. On the left, a tiny figure trudged away from the barn toward an ancient stone wall. It was lonely and beautiful at the same time.

"Oh!" Miko said, stopping at my elbow. "This is yours, Ms. Delacroix?"

"Yes," she said. "It is almost finished, but it is missing something. I cannot decide what."

Miko stood in front of the painting, taking it all in.

"What do you think, Miko?" Ms. Delacroix added suddenly. "What would you add if it were your painting?"

Miko thought about it for a moment. "I think," she said, "if it were mine, I might add one tiny splash of color. A little cardinal in one of the branches in the distance or something. But that's if it were me."

"It's a good suggestion," Ms. Delacroix replied. "But look how the time is getting away—let me pull up the submissions on my computer."

The computer screen was set up on a small table near the rack of canvases. Sitting next to the computer were five small notebooks and pens. Just as she'd said, the monitor was very large. Ms. Delacroix pulled several chairs over, then switched the monitor on and typed in the blog address.

"Twenty-two files," Ivy said, reading from the counter. "That's pretty respectable, guys."

"How do you want to go through them, Ivy?" Ms. Delacroix asked.

"Each one has a three-digit number randomly assigned by the computer," Ivy said. "So I'd say let's just scroll through them in order. Do you want me to do it?"

"Please," Ms. Delacroix said. "We'll change seats. Oh," she said as she pushed her chair toward Ivy. "And I put these aside for us."

She handed each of us a small new notebook and pen.

"So we can all keep track and make notes as we go through," she explained.

"Great," Ivy said. "I completely forgot to bring something to take notes with."

"I love the way new notebooks smell," Tally remarked. "There's something about the idea of all those blank pages—you could do anything with them. You could write a screenplay!"

"Or you could take careful notes," I suggested. "We have to all make sure we write the correct numbers down. Twenty-two pictures might not seem like a lot, but we need to keep track of our thoughts on every one and not get them mixed up."

"We're ready. Let's start," Miko said.

"Okay, here's the first new picture," Ivy said, clicking on a thumbnail. "The number is eight hundred and fifty-three."

Nobody said anything for a moment after the image appeared onscreen. It was a colored-pencil drawing of a fluffy animal—my guess was a guinea pig or a hamster. I didn't know what to say about it because the only thing I could think was that it wasn't very good. We all stared at the picture, the silence broken by the sudden rattling of windows as the wind picked up outside.

"That won't work as a cover image," Miko said briskly. "It just isn't right."

"I agree," Ivy said.

"But it's sweet that someone loves their hamster enough to draw him," Tally added.

"Eight hundred and fifty-three, guinea pig, won't work as cover," I read aloud as I wrote. After a minute, Tally scribbled something in her notebook, too.

"Okay, shall we move on to the next one?" Ms. Delacroix asked.

The next image was a photograph of an empty swing set, one I recognized from the elementary school playground. It was shot in black and white, the swing set appearing as a dark-gray blob against a blur of grass.

"Number three hundred and ninety-eight. I kind of like it as a photo," Ivy said. "But I don't think it makes enough of a statement to work on the cover. There's not really anything going on."

"I agree," I said as I wrote down the number and made a few notes.

"I'm not wild about it," Miko said.

"It's sad," Tally added. "The swing set looks abandoned. But it's nice someone liked the swing set enough to take a picture of it."

Was Tally going to find something nice to say about every single piece? *That's actually kind of sweet of her*, I thought.

"Okay, so we're passing on that one, too," Ivy said.

Only twenty left. The wind picked up again, making a low howling sound in the chimney. Outside the window, a spray of snow blew through the air.

As soon as the next image came onto the screen, I loved it.

It was a watercolor of a wooden door that stood half open. The foreground of the painting was very dark, but there was a brilliant light streaming through the open door that made a vivid contrast. Through the opening of the door, there was another small door visible, and that one was open, too, to reveal a black sky sparkling with stars.

"Wow," I said. "How did they do that?"

"This is pretty cool," Ivy said.

"It's great," Miko said, her pen poised over her notebook, her eyes on the screen. "For starters, it's well painted. But I love this idea, too—the first room is dark, the one beyond it is full of sunlight, and the one that's farthest away is full of starlight. The way this person achieved all these different light effects is really cool."

"And the doors are so mysterious," Tally added. "The way each one is partially opened."

"The doors look very realistic," I added. "They look like regular doors, like the ones in this house. But it's almost like the last room is in outer space. It could be scary, but the way it's been painted, it isn't. It's dreamlike."

"What number is this?" Miko asked. "I'm putting it down as a definite maybe."

"Seven hundred and fifty-six," Ivy read. "Okay. We'll come back and look at that one again."

The next couple of submissions were obviously not going to be picked, though no one came out and said it. One was obviously a joke—it was just a couple of stick figures with oversize smiley-face heads.

"Funny," Ivy said, shaking her head. "Wow, is that the wind?"

"Yes," Ms. Delacroix said, looking out the window. "It's gotten very strong."

153

"It sounds like a ghost when it comes down the chimney like that," Tally said, looking a little dreamy.

Miko's cell phone began to ring, and she answered it, her expression immediately turning to concern. She got up and moved a few feet away, and we all focused on the next picture, a photograph of the moon rising behind a massive fir tree. I copied the number down but couldn't decide what I thought of it, which probably meant it was a no.

"Okay, I will," I heard Miko say. She shut off her phone's ringer and gave us an apologetic look.

"Is everything okay?" Ms. Delacroix asked.

"Yes, except I'm going to have to go even earlier than I thought," Miko said. "I'm really sorry. That was my dad. He's been watching the local weather, and they've changed the forecast. He said the snow that was expected tonight is supposed to hit much earlier because it's been so windy—the front or whatever got here early. And now they're saying there is a high-wind warning in effect. He gets really anxious about stuff like that, and he's worried there will be some problem on the roads, and I won't make my coaching session. So he's driving over here now."

I glanced at my watch—it was barely one o'clock.

"Are you okay?" I asked Miko quietly.

"I'm fine," she assured me. "I don't mind going early." She actually seemed a little more relaxed. It occurred to me that Miko's father hadn't been the only one worrying about her getting to her final coaching session on time. Miko wanted to be here. But she wanted to be there, too.

"Anyway, it will take him twenty minutes to get here," Miko added. "So let's keep going. Are we done with the tree and the moon? That was four hundred and sixty-two, right?"

"Sure, let's move on," Ivy said.

There was another string of definite noes— paintings of dogs, photographs of shoes or clouds, a collage of what appeared to be lipstick ads. Tally said something nice about each one. There were so many I began to wonder if we'd seen all the best ones already. I counted nineteen in my notes, so that made for only three more. The twentieth was a watercolor of a rowboat, with a small shadowy figure at the helm, disappearing into a bank of fog and each oar creating a wake of ripples in the water.

"What number is this one?" I asked.

"Two hundred and eleven," Tally read. "I can't decide if I love it or it scares me. But I think it's good."

"Well, it could be both at the same time," Ms. Delacroix pointed out.

Really, it came down to this one or the open door. It was those two I had trouble picking between. The watercolor of the rowboat depicted something very real, but there was a magical, mysterious feeling I got from the little boat, being consumed by the fog. I wanted to know who was in the boat, and where they were going, and what was going to happen on the other side of the fog bank. But Tally was right— it wasn't necessarily a happy picture. There was something a little scary about it.

There was one more definite no, and the last picture was the one we'd already seen, of the safari balloon with the monkey hanging on to the string.

"And that's the last one," Ivy said. "Safari balloon is three hundred and ninety-six. How much time do you think you have, Miko?"

Miko checked the clock on her phone. "Maybe ten minutes. Can you scroll back through each one quickly?"

Ivy nodded, reading the number of each one aloud as she clicked through the images.

"Okay," I said suddenly. "I think I have an idea which ones I like best. So are we doing the judging anonymously, too?"

"No," said Ivy. "I don't see why we should. Let's just talk it through right now. So you go first, Paulie. Which one is your top pick?"

"The doorways," I said.

"And maybe each person say just a little bit about why," Ms. Delacroix suggested. "I will take notes, and we can include our comments or not, as you prefer, in the announcement and in the issue."

"Good idea," Ivy said.

"Okay, well, I picked the doors because first off I just think it's a really good painting. It's done well, and it catches my eye, and the more I look at it, the more interesting details I find. So for that reason I think that visually it would be great for the cover. But also, I feel like the painting isn't really about doors. To me it seems like it's almost a way of seeing into different worlds that are normally hidden, too. Or even seeing inside our own minds, and the things we close ourselves off to, if that makes sense."

There was silence as Ms. Delacroix scribbled some notes. I couldn't tell if she thought what I had said made sense or was confusing. No one said anything.

"Anyway, I like that one best. Someone else go now," I said.

"I'll go," said Tally. "My first pick is the watercolor of the rowboat. I like what's in it, but also, it makes me insanely curious about the story, like who the person in the boat is and what's going on," she said. "What's on the other side of that fog? Is there a really big boat there? Or a monster? And look how one oar is pulling into the water, but the other one is out, like the person is pulling the boat to the right. Are they turning around? The more I look at it, the more I want to know. I'm not even sure if the boat is coming out of the fog or turning to go into it."

"Cool," Ivy said. "Good eye, Tally. You almost have me convinced—but my favorite is still this photograph of the moon and the tree. I know it lacks some color, but on a cover, we could compensate with the type we choose. It's really simple and clean. It reminds me of summers in Maine, which I love. I don't know if that's a good reason to like it best, but that's how I feel."

"Sounds like a perfectly good reason to me," I said. I turned to ask Miko to give us her pick. She had gone over to the window facing the driveway and was watching for her dad's car.

"Ms. Delacroix? Have you decided on one?" I asked, trying to give Miko a little privacy—she was obviously getting more anxious.

"I have," she said, matter-of-factly. "Number two hundred and thirteen, the painting of the house with green shutters by a field. The composition is good, the perspective is well-executed, but mostly, like Ivy's moon, it reminds me of a place I love."

"Okay," Ivy said. "So we have four votes for four different pictures. Hey, Miko?"

Miko jumped slightly at the sound of her name.

"Sorry," she said, coming back to where we were sitting. "I thought I heard a car, but it was just the wind."

"It's okay," Ivy said. "We just need to know which of the submissions was your first pick, if you have one."

"I do," Miko said, looking at her notebook. "The number was . . . seven hundred and fifty-six. The house of doorways. It's just a striking visual image, which is obviously what we want for a cover. And I really like the technique. I think creating these different sources of light is really hard, and the painter did an amazing job."

"So then it has really been quite simple," Ms. Delacroix said. "We have two votes for the house of doorways. Is everyone happy with this winner?"

"I had it as number two," Tally said. "I think it's great."

"Well, it's definitely in my top two or three," Ivy said. "It will look beautiful on the cover. And since we had one vote each for three others, what do we think about announcing them as runners-up?"

"Love that idea," I said. "Miko?"

"Uh-huh, definitely," she said, shooting another quick look toward the window. When her phone rang, she jumped.

"Hello?"

"Okay," Ivy said to me. "We did it! Everything seems to be coming together."

"I thought that was exhausting," Tally said. "I

wonder if this is what it's like to be a casting director, looking at all those different people and deciding who you like and who you don't. It all makes me really hungry."

"Hungry?" asked Ivy. "I'm not seeing the connection."

"What's wrong? What happened?" I asked Miko. I had been watching her while she was on the phone. She was biting her lower lip, obviously distressed.

"My dad is calling from his car," she said. "A big tree has come down over this road, right near the turnoff from Route 21. He said there's no way around it. Ms. Delacroix, is there any other way to get here aside from Route 21?"

"Oh dear, Miko, I'm afraid there is not," Ms. Delacroix said. "This road doesn't go through—it ends just past my driveway."

"Dad? She says there isn't another way around. I . . . what? Oh. I see."

That didn't sound good.

"Okay. Okay," Miko said very quietly. She put the phone down.

"What if Ms. Delacroix drove you down the road to where the tree fell?" I asked, imagining Miko climbing over a fallen tree in the freezing cold with her violin in one hand. Probably not my best idea, I'll admit.

Miko shook her head.

"He said there are branches coming down all over the place, and they're saying on the radio the temperature is dropping really fast, and everything is starting to ice over. People are supposed to stay off the roads. He doesn't think it's safe."

I looked out the window. It was incredibly windy— I could see the branches of trees dancing around, and sprays of snow blowing through the air. It had gotten very dark outside.

"He's driving back home, and he said I should stay put. He said nobody should go anywhere."

Ivy's phone began ringing. "That'll be my mom," Ivy said. "She's probably glued to the Weather Channel, too."

As Ivy answered her phone, another gust of wind rattled the windows, and the image on the computer flickered, then disappeared.

"What happened?" Tally asked.

"Oh dear," Ms. Delacroix said. "Another power line must have come down. I'm afraid my electricity has gone out."

Okay, then. The day had just taken a very unexpected turn.

· chapter ·

12

I opened the front door and peered outside. The snow was falling hard and fast, and it looked like a few inches had already accumulated. I took a few steps out to get a better view, and it was as if I had walked onto a skating rink. Everything was covered in a glaze of ice. I skidded, pinwheeling my arms wildly, but slipped anyway. I landed on my butt and slid forward.

"Oh, are you okay?" Tally called anxiously from the doorway.

"I'm fine—it's like a skating rink out here!" I said, giggling. The first time I tried to get up, my feet just slipped again. Moving very slowly, I got up and reached the door, stepping inside with relief.

"Paulina, my goodness, that was quite a fall. Nothing is broken?" asked Ms. Delacroix.

"I'm fine, really," I said. "I just wanted to see how

much snow there really was. Everything is icing over. We could go skating!"

"I think you should come back in," Ms. Delacroix said.

"Me too," I agreed. "Brrr!"

"Come and sit by the fire," she said as I came back into the house, shivering.

It had been an hour since the electricity went off. Ivy's mother agreed everyone should stay put for the time being. My mother had called saying much the same thing.

Miko gave a heavy sigh, rubbing her hands together and frowning.

"Miko, are you still worrying?" I asked her. "I mean, it's all kind of out of our hands now, don't you think?"

It was three thirty. Miko had missed her coaching session, and it didn't look like any of us were going anywhere in the near future.

"This is all my fault," Miko said. "My dad didn't want to let me come today, but I absolutely insisted. I told him there was nothing I could accomplish by practicing this morning that was going to make or break my audition. He's going to be so upset. What was I thinking?"

She was thinking she was entitled to take a stand about something, I thought. And I was the one who suggested it. Had I made a mistake?

"Well, you couldn't help the weather," I said. "Could you have even gotten to the session if you'd stayed home?"

"The coach lives one street away from me," Miko said. "I could have walked. I'm only missing it because I insisted on coming here."

"Maybe it will be better if I talk to your father?" Ms. Delacroix offered.

Miko shook her head. "Thanks, but no. What's done is done."

"All right," she replied, changing the subject. "Is anyone hungry? Come into the kitchen, and we will find something to eat."

I felt terrible for Miko and tried to think what I could say or do to make it better as we followed Ms. Delacroix into the kitchen.

"It's still true, what you said, isn't it?" I asked Miko quietly. "About today not making any real difference one way or the other in the audition?"

"It might have been true about practicing this morning," she said. "But there were some things I was going to ask my coach. And any final advice, whatever she wanted to be freshest in my mind, she would have told me today. Now I'm missing that opportunity."

"Well, what if you called her?" I asked. "You could

at least ask your questions, right? And she could say anything she needed to tell you?"

Miko stopped in the doorway of the kitchen and looked at me. "I can't believe I didn't think of that," she said. "I mean, it won't help her show me anything or correct my playing, but I can ask her my questions. My cell is running a little low on juice, though."

"Use mine," I said. Mine wasn't full charged, either. I wanted to be able to text Benny if we were in fact stuck here—it would be fun to give him periodic updates and get messages from him. But this was more important. I handed Miko my phone.

"Take it in the other room if you want," I told her. "I'll get you a plate for when you're done."

The kitchen was small and cozy. Ms. Delacroix opened various drawers and pulled some things out of the refrigerator, and soon she had plates with cookies, cheeses, and crackers prepared. We each carried a plate into the living room—I carried Miko's, too—and got comfortable as Ms. Delacroix put another log on the fire.

"If I could eat one thing for the rest of my life, it would be cheese!" Tally exclaimed, taking another bite.

"For me it would be cupcakes," Ivy said.

"I'd want mashed potatoes," I said. "I could

definitely spend all eternity eating those."

"Let's hope you never have to test that theory," Ivy said, grinning. "Where's Miko?"

"She's calling her music coach with a couple of questions she was going to ask during the lesson," I said. Since Miko was out of the room, I might as well explain a little to our teacher.

"She's got this huge audition tomorrow for a summer program at the Music Conservatory," I explained. "She's been working really hard to get ready for it, and this was going to be her last session with the special coach she's been seeing."

"Ah, I see," Ms. Delacroix said. "Yes, she mentioned the audition, but I did not know it was coming so soon. Poor Miko—that is a stressful thing. I feel it is partly my fault—I should have checked the weather report more carefully. In storms this house is often without electricity, or the road is blocked if a tree falls or the creek floods. I did not think of that."

"Oh, but you couldn't have known," Tally said.

"The weatherman obviously knew," she replied. "But okay. We are here—we cannot change that now."

Miko came back into the room and handed me my phone.

"Thanks," she said, taking the plate I offered her and sitting down next to me.

"Did she answer your questions?" I asked.

"Yes," Miko said. "And she told me not to worry, that I will do fine. I just can't help feeling guilty, though."

"Well, we will do our best to distract you," Ms. Delacroix said. "Here, eat something."

• • • • • • •

By five thirty, after listening to the latest weather report on the radio, it was definite—we wouldn't be going anywhere until morning. Normally I would have found the entire situation hilarious—what a story it would make, trapped at our teacher's house because of a downed tree and a snowstorm that arrived six hours early. I sent Benny a text with the last of my battery.

> **News flash—the 4 Girls are stranded at Ms. Delacroix's house in a snowstorm with no electricity! Cell battery dying . . . so is the light . . . hope I survive the night, aghhh!!**

Miko was still unusually quiet, and I knew she was still feeling anxious. She had put so much time into preparing for this audition. Now she was stuck away from home the night before the big day.

"Are you worried you're going to have trouble sleeping?" I asked her while Ms. Delacroix and Ivy were in the kitchen trying to figure out what could be thrown together to make a dinner for five.

"Yeah, I kind of am," Miko said. "I'm just getting this bad feeling now, too. It's like everything that could go wrong is going wrong."

"No," I said firmly. "This is today. Tomorrow is a different day, and everything will be better. We'll wake up, the sky will be blue, the roads will be plowed, the tree will be cut up and cleared, and your dad will be here first thing to pick you up."

"You're right," Miko said. "But you might need to keep reminding me."

"No problem!" I assured her. "I've got all night."

"Well, I'm afraid all I can offer you for dinner is some spaghetti and a salad," Ms. Delacroix said, coming back into the room. "I have a gas stove that works even when the power is out. And I have some nice bread. But usually I make dinner only for one—so we don't have much to choose from."

"I love spaghetti," Tally said.

"So do I—that will be great," Miko added, trying to sound enthusiastic. She was probably too anxious now to want to eat anything at all. *Poor Miko.*

"Good," Ms. Delacroix replied, nodding with satisfaction. "And then, I suppose we can start thinking about where all of you will sleep. With so many trees down, it's quite likely the electricity

168

will not be coming back on tonight, and that unfortunately means the furnace cannot come back on. It will start to feel a little cold, so we should try to go to sleep early."

"Oh, let's all camp out by the fire!" Tally said. "It will be like part sleepover, part summer camp—except for the snowstorm. It would be so cozy—I've always wanted to sleep in a room with a fireplace. I mean, a fireplace with a fire in it."

"I think that is a good idea. This couch pulls out to be a bed big enough for two of you," Ms. Delacroix said. "And I have plenty of quilts and blankets and comforters to make a nice little nest on the floor for the other two. The fire will give some light and warmth."

"But what about you? Aren't you going to be freezing?" Miko asked.

"I will be warm enough in my own bed," Ms. Delacroix said. "I have gone plenty of nights here without power when there have been storms."

So it was official—we were stranded for the night. And school was sure to be canceled in the morning. Who would believe it when the four of us showed up at school on Tuesday and told everyone we had been snowbound with our new art teacher! It was definitely an adventure. If only it wasn't such a nightmare for Miko.

•   •   •   •   •   •   •

In the dark of night, the wind rattled at the windowpanes and howled down the chimney, where the fire was still burning cheerfully.

Ivy and Tally, who by virtue of a coin toss had ended up sharing the sofa bed, had both fallen asleep. Miko and I were lying head-to-head by the fire, talking quietly.

"The thing is, I feel bad that I've been complaining about my dad so much," Miko was explaining. "I mean, he has been pretty nuts about the audition, and he does push me hard on everything. But usually we get along just fine. He's a great cook. He always takes me to the movies or wherever I might want to go on the weekends. We usually have a couple of TV shows that we watch together, just him and me. It's just right now things are sort of tense between us. And when you add in the fact that Shelby and I aren't talking anymore, well, it's been kind of rough. I'm glad we've gotten to be such good friends," she told me quietly. "You've really been there for me these last few weeks, Paulie."

"I'm really glad we're friends, too," I told her earnestly. "So you really think this is it between you and Shelby?"

"I'm positive," Miko said. "She's barely said a word to me since that day she came and sat at our table, when she kept bringing up her submission. And she . . ."

"She what?" I asked.

Miko seemed to be struggling with something.

"Never mind," she said. "It doesn't matter—I shouldn't have brought it up. She does lots of strange things. It doesn't matter anymore. Because, I mean, I don't want to be friends with her anymore, I really don't. So I'm fine with it. But it's still, like, really sad."

"I understand," I said. "Do you remember Evelyn?"

"Sure," Miko said. "The girl who moved away at the end of last year. You guys were friends, right?"

"Best friends," I said. "I didn't know how I was going to get through seventh grade without her. And I still absolutely adore her. But we started off e-mailing each other every day when she moved and talking on the phone and Skyping. Now sometimes more than a week goes by, and I don't even think of her. And that kind of makes me feel sad, too. You and Shelby were close for a long time."

"Yep, up through last summer. There were times things started to feel strained this year. She definitely didn't like it that I was working with you guys on 4 Girls. Shelby has this thing where if she isn't part of something, she automatically wants to dump on it. It's like she has to prove that if she's not part of something, it's her choice because she thinks it's stupid."

"She's supercompetitive," I said. "And you're doing all this stuff she isn't—some of it she couldn't—your recital, *4 Girls*, this audition. Your art. Maybe that's why she's pushing her cover so hard—she wants to show that she can be artistic, too."

"Maybe that's part of it," Miko said. "And you're right—she's the most competitive person I've ever met. I don't have anything to prove to anybody. But she was weird about *4 Girls*, weird about my violin—she couldn't even bring herself to come to my recital, and then she made some incredibly lame excuse about it. And why? She thinks people think less of her because she doesn't play the violin? Or she didn't get offered an internship at *City Nation*? It's my life, not hers. Why can't she see that the only person comparing us is her? I just don't understand how her mind works."

"Me neither," I said.

"But she was a good friend to me, until this year," Miko said. "She really was. That doesn't all just go away because we've changed. And I mean, I kind of feel bad even talking about her now."

"Then we won't talk about her," I said.

"Thanks," Miko told me.

We both stared at the fire.

"I wish someone would just tell me what's going to

happen tomorrow," Miko said with a sigh. "You know, like, 'Miko, you'll do fine, but you won't get in.' Or, 'You'll make one big flub, but you'll get in, anyway.' It's so strange to think that soon I'll know. But it's all hanging over my head now."

I smiled at Miko's serious face. "You know, Miko, whatever happens at the audition, I just have this feeling deep down that you're going to be happy with it in the long run. It's strange, I just keep having this picture flash in my head, it's . . . oh, maybe I'm going loopy from being snowbound or something."

"What? What picture?" Miko pressed.

"Well, not actually a picture, just this sort of . . . image of you a long, long time from now, when you're, like, Ms. Delacroix's age. And you look different, but you're you. And you're living this amazing, creative life, and in that moment you're going to remember THIS night. Kind of like you're reaching out and waving to yourself across the years. Like through one of those doorways in the painting. Does that sound totally weird?"

"No, Paulina," Miko said, shaking her head. "It's beautiful. I'm going to remember that tomorrow when I'm on my way to the audition."

The wind picked up outside again, shaking the house and raging against the windows.

"Wow, I'm so tired," Miko said.

I think I said, "Me too." I might have just had time to think it, because suddenly I was utterly exhausted, too, and when I closed my eyes just to rest them for a moment, I slipped into a deep, comfortable sleep.

• • • • • • •

When I awoke the next morning, the first thing I registered was how cold it was with the fire out. The next thing I noticed was sunlight streaming through the windows and a clear blue sky outside. Someone was bustling around in the kitchen, whistling, and I heard voices and a familiar laugh. The sofa bed was empty, and I was the only one still in the living room.

I got up and went into the kitchen.

"Ah, here is our missing girl," Ms. Delacroix said cheerfully, dressed in a brightly colored robe and slippers.

"The power's back on! School is closed! And we're having French toast," Tally said, beaming. "All you need for that is bread, eggs, and milk, and Ms. Delacroix has it all!"

"Oh good—I'm starving," I said. "Miko, why do you have your coat on?"

"My dad's already on his way over," she said. "I called him as soon as I woke up—the phone is working again."

"You're sure you don't want to stay and have breakfast?" Ms. Delacroix asked. "Your father is welcome to join us."

"Thanks," Miko said. "But I'm so jittery, I really just want to get home and get myself as calm as possible."

"I understand," Ms. Delacroix said.

"I see a car," Ivy said. "Wait—there are two cars. My mom's here, too!"

Miko went right away, giving me a tight, quiet hug before she left hastily. We stayed long enough to gulp down some French toast while Ivy's mom chatted with Ms. Delacroix.

I felt a slight pang of regret at the thought of leaving the cozy house and going outside, though I was in yesterday's clothes and without so much as a hairbrush. Somewhere during the course of our stay, I realized I had forgotten to worry about what Ms. Delacroix thought of me. When it came time to say our thank-yous and good-byes, I was almost sorry to think of her being in the house all alone after we left.

But maybe she likes being alone, I thought as I climbed into Mrs. Scanlon's car. My mother always said painters and writers were the world's most solitary people.

My house was the first stop. My mother opened the front door before I even reached it.

"Here you are!" she exclaimed, opening her arms to hug me. "Can you believe that storm? I'm so relieved you all stayed put. That was not a storm to be out driving in."

Kevin shot down the staircase.

"Mom said you had to spend the night at a teacher's house!" he exclaimed.

"Yep—at my art teacher's house," I confirmed.

"Ew!" Kevin said.

I laughed. "Why *ew*?" I asked. "You don't even know Ms. Delacroix."

"But she's a teacher," Kevin said. "Going to a teacher's house is superweird, but sleeping over? Way scary!"

"Well, it wasn't *way scary*," I assured him. "Ms. Delacroix is a painter, and she lives in this beautiful old house. We got to sleep by the fireplace, and we had French toast for breakfast."

Kevin looked interested at the mention of French toast, but he still looked dubious at the suggestion that being stuck at a teacher's house could be anything short of a nightmare.

"So you had a good time?" my mother asked.

"It was fine," I told her. "But Miko missed her final music coaching session. She was kind of stressed about it."

"Oh dear," she said, shaking her head. "That's got

to be a lot of pressure. Poor Miko."

"I know," I said, following my mother into the kitchen. "But actually, I think she's going to be okay. Whatever happens, I mean. She seems to have some . . . what do you call it?"

"Perspective?" asked my mother.

"Yeah, perspective. I think she's got that now."

"Good," my mother said. "I hope you're right."

"Anyway, I'm gonna go take a shower and change," I said, starting toward the staircase.

"Oh, Paulina," my mother called, and I turned around.

"Yeah?"

"Benny's called twice this morning to see if you were home yet."

"Thanks," I said. "My cell phone died last night."

"Bennneeeeeeee!" sang Kevin, clasping his hands over his heart. "Bennneee Noooovaaaak! I just looooove hearing that naaaaame!"

He made a kissing sound, then staggered around pretending to throw up. Finally he seemed to get shot with some kind of invisible ray gun, and he slumped to the floor, tongue out, dead. I stepped over him and headed for the stairs.

I was in a good mood now, and I didn't care if Kevin made fun of me. Anyway, he was right.

I did love the sound of Benny Novak's name.

· chapter ·
13

I was trying to focus on school. It felt like a Monday, but it was really a Tuesday, and the teachers were pushing a little harder for us to make up work we had missed from the snow day. But I couldn't stop thinking about Miko. *She must be on her way to the conservatory right now for the performance portion of her audition.* She had specifically told me she had to leave school before lunch, and I was headed to the cafeteria now. Was she nervous? Or was she feeling confident now that yesterday's dreaded music theory was behind her?

I stopped at my locker to pick up the lunch my mother had packed for me and half skipped, half jogged to the cafeteria. I shot a look toward the big table near the milk dispenser where Benny usually sat—he was not there, nor were any of his friends. That meant they had a team meeting. Oh well. I'd see him later. Ivy was already at our usual table, her face buried in a book, sandwich in hand. She looked up, saw me, and smiled.

"Hey!" she said. "So did she go?"

"I didn't see her before," I said. "But she said her father was picking her up right before lunch. And you know his position on being late—so I'm sure they're on their way."

"Tell me again what she said last night," Ivy instructed.

I opened my brown bag and pulled out a sandwich. "Oh no," I said.

"What?"

"This is Kevin's lunch. We must have gotten them mixed up. Darn it—and I'm really hungry!"

"Well, you have a lunch," Ivy said. "Just eat that."

I tossed the sandwich, wrapped in foil and tucked inside a baggie, onto the table, where it landed with a thud.

"Do you have any idea what that is?" I asked.

Ivy shook her head.

"Salami and peanut butter," I told her.

"Oh, barf," Ivy said, breaking off half of her sandwich. "How did he talk your mother into that? Here, you better eat part of this."

"I'm not late!" Tally announced, bearing down on us like a charging rhinoceros.

"No, you are not," Ivy declared. "Today is a day that will live in the history books—the day Tally Janeway was on time."

"Did she go? Did I miss her?" Tally asked, sitting down heavily and pulling off her hat. The motion charged her hair with static electricity, and her curls seemed to be alive and trying to escape, floating in all different directions.

"Yep, we all missed her," Ivy said. "It's probably just as well. She looked so nervous this morning. A big good-bye-and-good-luck scene was probably the last thing she needed."

I sighed. "I just hope it goes well," I said. "Ugh. I don't want to think about it. So, Ivy, have you heard back from all our winners?"

Ivy grinned. "I have," she said. "Well, you guys know about Daisy, I told you that already. Our competition winner is very surprised and very happy. And I heard from the last runner-up last night—everyone has agreed to having their artwork reproduced in the magazine. The file is done. Ms. Delacroix made good on her promise to format and design the issue herself on her big superfancy computer, and the file is at the printer even as we speak."

"Wow!" Tally exclaimed. "I had no idea we got so much done so fast!"

"Amazing how that happens, isn't it?" Ivy said

with a grin. "Oh, so I got an e-mail back from the first runner-up, and I printed it out."

Ivy made a big production of pulling a piece of paper out of her bag and unfolding it meticulously.

"What?" I said, looking from Ivy to Tally. "What's going on?"

"I have no idea," Tally said. "But I usually don't."

"I present to you the e-mail from our first runner-up," Ivy said, "previously known only as number two hundred and eleven."

I took the e-mail from Ivy and looked at it.

▼ **To:** IvyNYC

▼ **From:** Submitter 211

▼ **Subject:** Cover Artwork

   Wow, I'm totally surprised. I'm glad you guys liked it, thanks!

"The name is at the bottom," Ivy pointed out.

"You are not serious," I said. "This is a joke, right? You made this, right, Ivy?"

"What?" Tally said.

"No joke!" Ivy said, beaming.

"What?" Tally asked again.

"The rowboat painting," I said, shaking my head

incredulously. "It's Benny's! Benny Novak!"

"Oh my gosh!" Tally squealed. "Your boyfriend is an artist!"

"Is that not amazing?" Ivy asked.

"I had no idea," I said. "No clue—I didn't even know he liked art. How could I not know that?"

"A lot of good artists came out of nowhere in this competition," Ivy said. "Look at Daisy. Who knew anything about her? The more I think about it, the more I think this competition was really a great thing— not just for *4 Girls*. For everybody."

"Benny Novak," I murmured, still shaking my head. "Wow. But that painting was so good!"

"Do yourself a favor," Ivy suggested, grinning. "When you talk to Benny, try not to sound so surprised when you say that!"

I laughed. "No, I know! I just . . . wow. This is so cool!"

"What's so cool?"

I turned around and gave a guilty jump, folding the paper in half. I hadn't noticed Shelby coming up behind me.

"Nothing," I said. "We're just . . . this is our wrap-up meeting for the issue."

"So who's the big winner? Who are the runners-up?" Shelby asked.

"Like it says on the blog," Ivy said, with exaggerated

patience, "that stays a secret until the issue is printed and handed out. You'll just have to wait until Friday, like everyone else."

"But what about the artists? Have you contacted them, or is that part a surprise, too?" Shelby pushed.

That part of the process wasn't necessarily a secret. But what Shelby wanted to know was if she'd made it into the top four. She wanted to push us into telling her on the spot.

This is our celebratory moment, I thought. *She doesn't get to ruin that.*

"You'll just have to wait until Friday," I said.

"That's moronic," Shelby said, scowling at me.

"Did you even talk to Miko this morning?" I asked. I felt a little bad that she'd baited me into being competitive with her, but this time I couldn't help it. "You know she's at her audition right now."

Shelby rolled her eyes. "Please. If I never hear one more word about that stupid audition or her stupid violin . . . Whatever—have fun with your little surprise. Enjoy your little moment of power. People are, like, so over it already."

She turned on her heel and marched off.

"Man," Ivy said. "Is it me or is she just getting meaner?"

I sighed. "It's getting pretty bad," I said. "She and Miko are pretty much not speaking."

"Good," Ivy said. "I'm sorry if that sounds harsh, but Miko's way better than that. I don't think Shelby's a good friend for her."

"I have to agree with that," I said. "But that doesn't mean ending the friendship doesn't hurt."

"Paulina, there he is!" squealed Tally as Benny Novak poked his head through the cafeteria doorway.

About twenty people were looking around to see who Tally was pointing at, but I didn't care.

Benny Novak was my boyfriend, and his painting had made it into *4 Girls*! At the moment, I didn't care if the entire world knew it!

"Hey, guys, do you mind if—"

Ivy made a grand gesture, shooing me away. "Go," she said. "Congratulate him for all of us. And leave my sandwich here."

I laughed. "Thanks. Catch you guys later!"

He smiled when he saw me coming and ducked back into the hall.

"Hey," I said. "I just this second found out. I can't believe you—that painting was unbelievable!"

"I figured when I got Ivy's e-mail you didn't know yet," he said, grinning.

"No, she just told me just now," I said. "Let's walk to our lockers—it's too noisy in the cafeteria."

"Okay, so you have to, like, tell me the brutal, honest truth about it," Benny said, giving me an intent look.

Those eyes!

Get ahold of yourself, Paulina, I thought sternly.

"Benny, we picked you. Completely anonymously. Yours was absolutely and positively one of the best."

"Okay, I get that," he said, grabbing my arm. "But . . . oh man, I feel really stupid for even asking, but . . . I mean, were there a lot of submissions? Or did you get, like, seven, and you picked the best four, and the other three were all, like, crayon drawings of kittens and stuff?"

I laughed and shook my head.

"No, it wasn't like that at all," I said. "We got over twenty submissions. It took us over an hour—we went through each one. There's probably a bunch of stuff I'm not supposed to tell you, but I will say this—as soon as we saw yours, everyone agreed it was one of the best—we thought that even before we'd seen the rest of them. Seriously. Benny, it's a really great painting!"

Benny looked relieved. "Okay—don't tell me anything else," he said. "That's all I wanted to know. I mean, I've never tried to do anything like that before. And I thought it might be good. And then I thought, *Nah—it couldn't be that easy*!"

It was funny. Benny always seemed so confident to me. And I thought I knew every little thing about him. But it turned out he had worried just as much about our relationship as I had. And he worried that this incredible painting he'd done might not be that good—when it was just so amazingly obvious that it was great!

I guess everybody has doubts about themselves, I thought. The next time my Anxiety Blob took over, I had to remember that.

"But it was that easy," I said to him.

He gave me a planet-tilting smile and slipped his arm through mine. "I guess sometimes things just are what they are," he said. "Nice necklace, by the way."

I gave him a planet-tilting smile right back.

"Well, thank you," I said. "My boyfriend gave it to me."

· **chapter** ·

14

Early Friday morning we had a stack of boxes packed with the newly printed fourth issue of *4 Girls* magazine loaded into Mrs. Scanlon's car. Miko, Tally, and I were in the backseat and Ivy was in the front as Mrs. Scanlon sat with us waiting for the school to open. Mrs. Scanlon was listening to the morning news on the radio as we chattered away to each other. Each of us had a copy of the magazine on our laps.

"Do you think we should have sized the three runner-up pieces larger?" Ivy asked, turning halfway round in her seat to look at Miko.

"No, I don't think you could have at that DPI—they wouldn't have reproduced as clearly," Miko said, flipping through the pages. "This size is perfect. And the whole section of letters and contributions people sent in is laid out really well. What program did you use?"

"Ms. Delacroix did it," Ivy told her. "I would have figured something out, but when she realized you'd normally be the one doing the layout, she offered. Said it would be a snap on her computer."

"Cool," Miko said.

Miko started to say something else, but it was lost in the sound of Tally struggling through a massive, drawn-out yawn.

I have never heard an explanation for why yawns are contagious, but before Tally's mouth was even closed I was yawning, too, then Miko.

"Oh, sorry, y'all," she said. "I'm gonna put everyone to sleep—I just can't help it. I don't even understand what a yawn is. It looks weird and feels weird and sounds weird, and after I've started yawning, I have to keep yawning, but all it does is make me feel more tired, not less tired, so I don't know why I do it, but I can't—"

She stopped midsentence and yawned, which immediately contaminated me.

"Uh-oh, it's escalating," Ivy said, cracking herself up. She alone was immune to the yawning—even her mother was starting to do it as she listened to the news. The rest of us must have looked ridiculous to anyone happening to glance into the car.

"Did you guys ever wonder why we have a

word for *sneezing* and a word for *belching* but no word for *yawning*?" Ivy asked.

"Isn't the word just *yawn*?" Tally asked. She promptly yawned again.

"Tal, no more!" Miko said, covering her face with her hands. "When are they going to unlock that door?"

The plan was for the four of us to be stationed around school before the first bell, handing out the magazine. The school was usually open by seven, with students arriving at seven thirty, but for some reason today they were running a few minutes late letting us in.

"I hope you get some news today, Miko," I said.

"Me too," she replied. "It would be nice to know before the weekend."

"And they wouldn't even give an estimate, like, you'd hear in around two days or a week?" Ivy asked.

Miko shook her head. "Nope. Nothing."

"That seems so rude," Tally said. "Making you wait like that. They do exactly the same thing in the theater, Miko. When I was waiting for the cast list for *Annie* to go up in October, I thought I was going to lose my mind. And that was only one part in a school play."

"Hey, look, somebody's unlocking the front door," Ivy said, pointing. "Good, so we can go in."

"Okay, everybody ready? Let's go!" I said.

Tally gave a reluctant look out the window. "But it's so cold out there," she said. "Every single day it seems like it's even colder than the day before."

It was true. The three-week cold snap had been a big news story on its own. It was the coldest stretch of weather on record in our county in 150 years.

I threw my door open, letting a blast of icy air into the car.

"Better get it over with as quick as possible, then," I said. "Come on!"

It WAS bitterly cold outside the car. The air sliced into my lungs painfully. Mrs. Scanlon popped the trunk, and we each grabbed a few of the cartons that held our new issue. Ivy somehow managed to close the trunk with her elbow.

"Thanks!" we called to Mrs. Scanlon. No one wanted to linger in the parking lot, so we set off toward the front door as fast as we could with the boxes in hand.

"See, it's nice and warm in here," Ivy said once we were inside. "I think they keep it a little too warm sometimes."

Tally went into the office to sign us in early, while we opened the cartons and pulled out stacks of magazines.

"It really does look fabulous," I said. "I think it might be a tie with the first-issue art Miko did for best cover ever."

"Oh please, this is much better than my cover," Miko declared.

"I can't get over the fact that not one of us even knew who Daisy Ford was," Ivy said, tracing her finger over the print on the cover.

WINNER OF THE *4 GIRLS* COVER COMPETITION: *DOORWAYS* BY DAISY FORD

"Well, she is new this year," I said. "And she is an eighth-grader."

"Yeah, well, *I* was new this year, too," Ivy reminded me. "September seems, like, forever ago."

"You can say that again," Miko said.

"Tally said Audriana rides the bus with Daisy, and she's super, unbelievably shy," I added. "I hope this will be a good thing for her."

"When I talked to her on the phone, she said she was over the moon about winning—superpsyched," Ivy said.

"Well, I hope she likes the finished product," I said, admiring the stacks I had made of magazines.

"What's not to like? It's gorgeous!"

"I signed us in early, y'all," Tally said, coming back holding a roll of bright-orange duct tape in one hand.

"Oh, look at the stacks—they look so professional! Where should I go?"

"What's the tape for?" I asked.

Tally looked at her hand, and her mouth dropped open in surprise. "I have no idea," she said. "It was on top of the clipboard—I forgot I was holding it! I'll go put it back!"

She rushed back into the office.

"That was random," Ivy remarked with a smile. "Okay, what's the plan here?"

"Well, if you and I handle the main door for the bussers, Miko and Tally could go to the playground entrance where the walkers come in."

"Cool," Miko said.

"Okay, I'm back," Tally said, sprinting back from the office and grabbing a carton. At least she seemed past her fit of yawning. The roll of orange tape was now around her forearm like a huge bracelet.

"You're with me, Tal," Miko said. "Come on— we're working the playground door."

"Yay! See y'all in art class!" Tally sang to me and Ivy, trotting off happily alongside Miko.

"Have fun!" I called. "Huh, there's a car pulling up out front—somebody else is coming in early."

Ivy peered out the door, then groaned.

"It's Shelby," she said. "Doesn't she usually go on the bus? What's she doing here early?"

"She knows we're handing out the issue this morning," I said. "I'm betting it has something to do with that."

Shelby caught sight of us the second she came through the front door. She took a copy of *4 Girls* without a word, looked at the cover, then opened it and flipped through the pages so hard I thought she might have torn one or two of them. Then she stared at us, one hand on her hip.

"Seriously?" she asked. "Not even one of the three runners-up?"

I could not believe Shelby was confronting us over not being picked. Who did that?

"Shelby, we had a ton of entries," I said. "A lot of them were really good."

Shelby shook her head angrily. "No, you guys are totally full of it, and I just proved it," she said. "I'm going to kill Miko when I see her. I knew she was going to make this personal."

"What are you talking about?" Ivy asked her.

"Miko has been blowing me off for weeks. Apparently, if you don't play the violin or get offered design internships or get perfect grades, you're not good enough for her anymore. When I heard about this competition, I decided to see if Miko would use it to try to get back at me. I found a professional piece of art, from somebody who got an art degree and won prizes and all that, and I figured if Miko knew it was my submission and it still didn't win, then I would know that Miko kicked me out of the running just to be spiteful."

"Whoa, wait a minute," I said, standing up and putting my stack of magazines down. "Shelby, are you saying you took a professional artist's work and submitted it as your own? That's cheating!"

"No, it isn't," Shelby said defiantly. "That's me proving that you're cheating. Because if you ended up picking some middle-schooler's illustration over a professional one, then you're either incredibly stupid and don't know what you're doing, or you're using the magazine to reward people you like and punish people you don't. Benny Novak is a runner-up? Your boyfriend? Oh, big surprise there. You guys are totally the ones who are cheating."

I was so angry with Shelby I wanted to scream. Ivy's face was turning red with anger, too.

"Do you have any idea the position you would have put us in if that image had been chosen to be on the cover?" Ivy asked. "How foolish we would have looked? Not to mention it being a copyright violation—we could have gotten in trouble."

"Yeah, but my whole point is you didn't pick it," Shelby declared. "Which proves that you guys have no idea how to judge an art competition. And since

Miko was the head judge, that makes her the biggest faker out of all of you!"

I suddenly realized what all this was actually about. It was like Miko thought—Shelby took all of Miko's accomplishments personally, as if they were some kind of judgment on her. And every time Miko had a recital or an audition or anything like that, Shelby could only see it as a mark against her personally. Shelby wanted to prove Miko wasn't as much of an artist as she thought, or something like that. I was still a little angry, because like Ivy said, it could have created a big problem for us if we'd put a stolen image on the cover of *4 Girls*.

But we hadn't. And what Shelby had done was sad. She was losing Miko as a friend and she knew it, and this was her bizarre way of doing something about it.

"Look, Shelby, I'm sorry, but you're just wrong," I said. "We all cast a vote for the piece we liked best. And it wasn't just us. We have a faculty adviser now—Ms. Delacroix, the new art teacher. She voted, too. If you feel like the process wasn't fair, you're welcome to go and talk to her about it. But she'll tell you the same thing I'm telling you now. And while you're at it, tell her you submitted someone else's work and passed it off as your own. I wonder how she'll feel about that. Seems to me like the only person using this competition as a weapon was you."

Shelby opened her mouth, then closed it, making an irritated sound. "Where's Miko?" she demanded. "I want to talk to her."

"She's with Tally," Ivy said. "Leave her alone. Have you even asked her how her audition went? If you are really her friend, you should care about that stuff."

"Haven't you heard anything I just said? She's not my friend," Shelby stated. "Not anymore. I'm done with her. And there's nothing she can say or do that will change my mind."

She spun on her heel and stalked off, leaving me and Ivy staring at each other in astonishment.

"I'm not even sure what the most unbelievable part of that was," Ivy said.

"Me neither," I said, shaking my head. "I actually feel kind of sorry for her. This is all about Miko—she's been convinced that Miko basically judges her for NOT being all the things she is, which is ridiculous. I'm not an artist or a violinist or anything, either, but I know Miko is my friend. It's like she had to come up with some huge, overblown reason to dump Miko, and this is it."

"It is sad," Ivy said. "But I'm also really angry about it. What are we supposed to do, just forget about it? Turn her in? She cheated!"

"I'm not sure," I said. "But I'd love to talk to Miko about this before Shelby finds her. Do you think you can man the door by yourself?"

"Of course I can," Ivy said. "Go! I'll be fine!"

• • • • • • •

There were already some students coming in through the playground entrance, but just a few. I asked Tally, who somehow seemed to STILL be holding the roll of orange duct tape, to pass out magazines by herself for a few minutes. She enthusiastically agreed.

Miko followed me into the stairwell. "What's up?" she asked.

"Listen, I just saw Shelby. She came in just now and marched right over to me and Ivy without a word and grabbed a copy of *4 Girls*. And when she saw she hadn't even made one of the runners-up, she lit into us. Into you. And you won't believe what she was saying."

Miko sighed. "She submitted a piece by a professional artist that has won some awards, and since we didn't choose it, we're either stupid or out to get her, probably both," Miko said.

"Wait . . . basically, yes! Wait, did you know about this?"

"I wasn't sure exactly what she was up to, but I

knew it was something like this. I recognized the safari balloon picture when it came in—I knew it looked familiar. Finally I just did a Google image search and found it. Type in 'monkey with a balloon' and up it comes. Meanwhile Shelby was going out of her way to let me know she was the one who submitted it. I figured the only possible reason was it was some kind of test to see what I would do. I almost told you guys, but . . . I don't know. If anyone had voted for it, I would have. I just didn't know what to do—it was all muddled in my head."

"No, it's fine," I said. "I totally understand."

"Ivy is probably mad, though," Miko said. "She is, isn't she?"

"She's certainly mad at Shelby," I said. "But the thing she was most upset about was what would have happened if we'd run the picture not realizing it was someone else's work. But you knew, and you wouldn't have let us do that. So I think that will make her feel much better."

"Good," Miko said. "It was just too much, you know? I didn't want to deal with it. But I did tell Ms. Delacroix about it."

"You did?" I asked, surprised.

"Well, yeah," Miko said, looking a little embarrassed. "I hope that was okay. I felt like I couldn't just keep it to myself—I would have worried then. But she said however I wanted to handle it would be okay with her. So I felt better knowing that she knew."

"I'm really glad," I said. "When you first said you wanted her to be our faculty adviser, I was kind of worried. I didn't know how we'd all get along, or if she would try to change things, or if we could even work together. To be honest, she made me really nervous. I worried that she'd think I did things like a total amateur or something. It seems silly now. What's strange is it was just now that it really came clear to me because of Shelby."

"Because of Shelby?" Miko asked.

"Yeah," I said. "She's just so far off base, thinking that you were judging her for not being like you—it was so obvious to me. But that's kind of what I was doing with Ms. Delacroix, not to mention the whole Benny thing. I let my insecurity get the better of me. What does Ms. Delacroix care if I'm not a painter or a designer or whatever she's been? I'm *me*. I guess that's the thing with Shelby—she's a PQuit and everything, I mean, she's THE PQuit. But she also really insecure with who she is."

"Yeah, she is," Miko agreed. "She hides it really well. But deep down she is very insecure, and it's not getting better, it's getting worse. But I can't help her with that. Not right now."

"Nope, you can't," I told my friend. "You've got enough going on in your own life."

The halls began to fill with the sound of voices.

"Here they come, our faithful readers," I said. "Shall we go see how the latest issue is going over?"

Miko smiled. "I'm ready if you are," she said.

I had my hand on the handle of the stairwell door when Miko's phone buzzed. I waited as she checked a text. She stood perfectly still, staring at the phone intently. Then she typed a quick response and turned her phone off.

"Sorry," she said. "That was my dad."

I froze, my hand still on the door handle. "Okay?" I said carefully.

Miko took a deep breath. "The mail just came, and my mother called him. I told them if something was delivered while I was at school they should just open it."

"Okay," I said again.

"And I got in."

I let the words sink in for a moment. I wanted to make absolutely sure I had heard her right. "The conservatory accepted you?"

Miko looked at me almost as if I was the one breaking the news to her.

"They accepted me," she said. "I'm in. I'm in!"

"Miko! That's amazing!" I exclaimed. I hugged

her, and she started to laugh.

"It doesn't seem real," she said through her laughter. "It doesn't seem real at all. I mean, I read his text, and I didn't feel anything at all. I think I'm starting to feel something now, though."

"It's too big to be real right away," I said, letting go of her. "It's huge news—you have to let it sink in! Your parents will probably want to celebrate tonight, right?"

Miko tucked her hair behind her ear and bit her lip. "Yeah, but . . . yeah. I'm sure I'll have decided by then."

"Decided what?"

"If I'll be going," she told me.

"If you'll be going? But I thought your dad just told you that you got in," I said, confused. Had I misunderstood her after all?

"He did," she said. "That's my official invitation to attend the summer program. Now I have to decide if I'm going to accept it."

I must have been making an extremely confused face because Miko took one look at me and burst into laughter.

"Don't worry," she said. "I'm ninety-nine percent sure I'm going to go. Maybe it's stupid, but I just kind of want to feel like I'm taking the time to decide, you know?"

"No, of course!" I said. "Now you know you CAN go, and you need to make sure it's what you WANT to do. That makes total sense."

The door to the stairwell opened, and three eighth-grade girls rushed through. They were all holding copies of *4 Girls* and chattering to each other, and they hardly seemed to notice us.

"No, I totally knew Daisy could paint," one of them was saying. "I absolutely, totally knew."

"Whoops, I got two," said the second girl as the group started up the stairs. "Hey—did you guys get one of these?"

I caught the copy of *4 Girls* that the girl tossed my way as she trotted up the stairs with her friends.

"Did someone just give us their extra copy of our own magazine?" Miko asked.

I laughed, holding it up. "It does look really great," I said.

"I kind of feel like this now," Miko said, pointing to the cover. "Like I'm standing where Daisy is painting from. And there are doors everywhere. Doors leading to doors that lead to more doors."

"I know what you mean," I said. "Me too."

It was a good feeling. Things were happening. They were happening for Miko and for *4 Girls* and for Benny and for me. And one thing had a way of leading to the next before you knew it. Miko had so much to look forward to. We all did. It was good to take the time to look around and appreciate the moment right now.

Because you never knew when another door was going to open or where it might lead.

ABOUT THE AUTHOR

Elizabeth Cody Kimmel is a widely published author of thirty books for children and young adults, including *The Reinvention of Moxie Roosevelt* and the *Suddenly Supernatural* and *Lily B.* series. Elizabeth is proud to admit that she was never asked to sit at the Prom-Queens-in-Training table in her middle-school cafeteria. She likes reading, hiking, peanut butter cups, and *Star Trek*, but not at the same time. You can visit her at www.codykimmel.com.

see how 4 Girls began in:

forever FOUR

· chapter ·

1

Who gets in trouble when it's only the second day of school?

Not me. But the kid sitting across from me outside the principal's office was definitely in trouble. I could tell by the way he was hanging his head and scowling at his sneakers. I tried to act like I didn't notice him because this was a very big day for me. I'd been getting ready for it for half the summer. If everything went well with Principal Finley, I might be about to change my entire life.

I started rereading my notes from the beginning, even though I pretty much had them memorized. It was my Big Idea, my shot at seventh-grade fame, my chance to change the world. Well, maybe not the entire world right away. But at least the gym, and maybe the cafeteria. All thanks to a little competition offered by the Curriculum Education Project.

What's the Big Idea, you might ask? A magazine for middle-school girls. Written by me. From the ins and outs of the schoolhouse to the White House, I was going to cover it all. What to expect on the overnight field trip. What to expect on the state tests. What to expect from college in five years and from global warming in ten years. The magazine was going to be new and different and undeniably Me. I absolutely could not wait to get started. All I had to do was make a killer presentation, better than anyone else who'd entered a project in the competition.

The troublemaker heaved a giant sigh, and I glanced over at him. I kind of knew who he was— Alan Something-or-other. He was a year ahead of me, spazzy, and perpetually over sugared. I wondered what he'd done this time. Last year he snuck a plastic cockroach onto the faculty cookie tray. From what I heard, it caused quite a scene. Teachers still inspected each chocolate-covered treat for signs of life before taking a bite.

Alan caught me looking and gave me a glare, so I shifted my gaze to the bust of George Washington by the door. I gave our Founding Father a little wink. I feel like George Washington would be psyched about my plans to change the world with my magazine. I'll bet he would have been Team Paulina all the way.

The door to the hallway flew open with a bang, and I jumped with a guilty start. Nobody wants to be caught winking at the bust of a departed president. But the girl with wild, blond curls barreling through the doorway didn't seem to notice. She fixed her enormous blue eyes on me and placed one hand over her chest.

"There is a *bat* in the music room!" she exclaimed breathlessly. "A crazed bat! I saw it with my own eyes, and it tried to attack me! I barely got out of there alive!"

Tally Janeway. She was Theater Club Royalty. A bubbly explosion of drama usually surrounded her, like a can of Coke someone's little brother had shaken up. The bigger the drama, the bigger Tally's southern accent grew. Right now, it was as thick as icing.

"A bat?" I asked. Alan folded his arms across his chest and made an "I Am Ignoring You Both" face.

Tally nodded and started pacing the room.

"I know, right?" she said. "In the music room! And it came right at me—all flappety wings and pointy teeth. I'm tellin' you, that bat wanted me *dead*!"

Tally drew out the last word—*dayyyudddd*. She stared at me, her eyes huge, waiting for my reaction.

I wasn't really sure what to say. She *might* actually have been chased by a murderous bat, but knowing Tally, it was also more likely she'd just seen a very large bee.

"That sounds crazy," I said. So crazy, I wasn't sure how else to respond.

Tally stopped pacing and pointed a finger at me.

"Paulina, that is *exactly* what it was. Cuh-razy. Hey, am I late?"

Tally and I were friendly enough, but we weren't actually *friends*. So I had no idea if she was late or not. I didn't even know why she was here.

"Well," I said carefully. "I guess that depends on what you're here for."

"Paulina Barbosa, that is deep," Tally declared. She fixed Alan with a look, like she was expecting him to weigh in on my unexpectedly philosophical observation. He just folded his arms tighter and closed his eyes.

Tally plunked herself down in a chair and immediately looked sleepy. When she was right in the middle of a huge yawn, the door opened again.

Miko Suzuki walked into the room. I gulped. While Tally was regular-people popular, Miko was Big-Time Popular. Tally knew my name and talked to me every once in a while. Miko knew my name and pretended I didn't exist. If I had to make a list of people I was afraid to rub the wrong way, Miko Suzuki would definitely be on it. She and her friends could turn your life into a nightmare if they got mad at you. Ask Suzie Gunderson, who made the World-

Class Mistake of laughing out loud when Miko accidentally sat on a cupcake during the fifth-grade Christmas pageant rehearsal. After that incident, Suzie endured four solid months of finding icing spread on her stuff, including her hairbrush. It was enough to turn a person off from cake for a very long time.

I looked at Miko without seeming like I was looking at her—a little trick I've gotten good at over the years, since it's never a good idea to initiate eye contact with someone like Miko. People have gotten their lockers toilet papered for less.

Miko was picture-perfect, as always. What did she do to get her hair to look so smooth? How did her lip gloss stay on so evenly, without any smudged to one side?

I sighed quietly.

Miko hung out with the other picture-perfect girls I secretly called Prom-Queens-in-Training. PQuits. The pecking order was very clear. I was sort of a Brain. And Brains weren't supposed to say hello to PQuits without the PQuits saying it first. Unless they were looking for trouble. And I did. Not. Like. Trouble. So I didn't say anything at all.

Miko glanced at me, then looked at Tally. Alan was apparently completely invisible.

"Hi, Tally," she said, taking a seat exactly halfway between the two of us.

"Hey, Miko," Tally responded brightly. "Did you hear about the bat in the music room?"

"I heard it was a mouse," Miko said.

"It was a *bat*," Tally corrected her. "A huge one. I'm pretty sure it bit me. I could have rabies, y'all. I could turn into a vampire!"

As Tally rambled on about the size of the bat's fangs, how long it took the average girl to become a vampire, and whether vampire bats and vampires were actually the same thing, Miko looked at me again. It seemed like she was trying to decide whether to say hello. Or whether she knew my name. Or if I was a Brain or an Outcast. It was all an act, though. Miko and I had been at the same school since kindergarten. She knew exactly who I was—she was just pretending not to remember. Classic PQuit move.

". . . or garlic around my neck, but it would smell sooo bad, or a stake through the heart, which is so funny, y'all, because when I was little I thought it meant a *steak* through the heart, like meat, right? And I couldn't ever understand how you could get a steak through a . . ."

Tally's words came faster and faster until they all seemed to run together. Miko rolled her eyes.

"Tal, enough already," Miko said. "You're frying my brain, and I have to concentrate when I go in there to talk to Mrs. Finley."

I suddenly wondered what Miko was doing here. While Tally might or might not be in trouble, PQuits never broke school rules. Or at least they never got *caught* breaking them. So why did Miko need to talk to the principal?

Before I could come up with any theories, the door to the principal's office opened. I stood up as Mrs. Finley came into the waiting area. She was wearing her usual, sensible dark suit, and her graying hair was sculpted into an impeccable bun.

"Good morning, everyone," Mrs. Finley said. She didn't look surprised to see that there were four of us waiting for her. "Alan, you will need to wait a little longer," she said firmly. "I have a scheduled appointment right now."

Something fluttered in my stomach. This was it— the moment I'd been waiting for since July. I walked into the office and sat down in the big chair closest to the desk. I did have a scheduled appointment after all. Miko and Tally would have to wait with Alan.

But to my surprise, Miko and Tally followed me inside. *What were they doing?* This wasn't like open mic night—you couldn't just waltz right in, even if you were a PQuit. I looked at Mrs. Finley, trying to send her a telepathic message that Miko and Tally were not part of my presentation.

But Mrs. Finley didn't say anything. She simply sat down at her desk and pulled out some papers. Then she glanced up to smile at all three of us.

"Let's get started," she said. "You're here because of the applications you have completed for the student competition called the Curriculum Education Project. It's very exciting that this program is available to fund a new student group specifically for girls. As you're obviously aware, we've lost a number of organizations and clubs because of budget cuts. The CEP is giving us a chance to get something back."

I knew all of this. It was all in the package we'd gotten over the summer from the CEP. The most important part was the prize—the project that won would get full funding for an entire year. I felt like my magazine was exactly what they were looking for, and I had a good shot at winning.

"We've had a wonderful response from the middle-school students," Mrs. Finley continued. "I received more submissions than I expected. I distributed all of them to the faculty and school board, and we have selected what we feel are the four ideas that have the most potential."

I peeked at Tally and Miko. So they must have submitted CEP ideas, too. I could imagine Tally wanting to do something theater related. But what kind of idea would a PQuit have come up with?

"Four of the proposals I received were very similar," Mrs. Finley continued. "That is why I have asked to meet with you girls as a group. I'm hoping you'll be able to work as one."

I blinked. *Work as a group? Oh no.* That was not one of my strong suits. Since kindergarten, my otherwise pretty excellent report cards always included the comment "Does not work well in groups."

Mrs. Finley placed four file folders on the desk.

"All of your proposals were for some kind of student publication written and published by girls, for girls. Both the faculty and school board loved the idea. I'd like you to work together on it."

I felt my face flush. This couldn't be happening. This was MY Big Idea! How could other people have come up with the same thing? Especially *these* people? I couldn't work with a drama queen and a Prom-Queen-in-Training. Tally was nuts, and Miko wouldn't even acknowledge my existence!

I could just say no, I thought. Tell Mrs. Finley that I changed my mind about the project. But I had put so much work into it. I was so sure I could do something amazing, make a splash, and change the world. I had even told some people about it—possibly even bragged a little. It would be so humiliating to end up quitting before I even got started.

And something told me Mrs. Finley wasn't asking if I was okay with it. She was telling me I would be. Me, Tally, and Miko would be working together on the magazine as a group. Like it or not.

I did not.

"So your group will be one of the four finalists. The CEP guidelines allow each group a trial period of one month."

"Like an audition?" Tally asked.

Mrs. Finley nodded.

"Exactly," she said. "You will write and publish the first issue of a magazine. You must do all the work yourselves and not get any help from your parents or other professionals. You'll have a budget of one hundred dollars for any costs. The final project will be judged by a faculty and student vote."

A million thoughts rushed through my head. How would I do my magazine my way with people like Miko and Tally tossed into the mix? The whole thing was ridiculous.

There was a knock on the door.

As I heard Mrs. Finley call "Come in," I remembered she said she had received *four* similar proposals. But there were only three of us here.

I glanced over at Miko, who had turned toward the door. From where I was sitting I couldn't see who was about to come in, but apparently Miko could.

She was scowling for all she was worth.

Wow. Who had earned a PQuit scowl this early in the morning? Even I had just been ignored.

My curiosity got the better of me, and I leaned forward to get a good look.